THE MYSTERY OF THE 99 STEPS

NANCY DREW's search for a flight of 99 steps to solve the mystery of a friend's weird dream takes her to France. But before she leaves the United States, an unknown person calling himself Monsieur Neuf warns the young sleuth not to pursue her mission.

With her friends Bess and George, Nancy arrives in Paris to join her father who is working on another case: to find out what, or who, is frightening wealthy financier Monsieur Leblanc into selling large amounts of securities.

Startling discoveries convince the young detective that Mr. Drew's case and her own mystery are linked by the 99 steps, and that a mysterious Arab has a strong hold over Leblanc. Is it blackmail? she wonders.

Nancy's quest for further clues leads to the romantic chateau country in the Loire Valley, where a web of danger closes in tightly around the three girls. How Nancy unearths the exciting mystery of the 99 steps will hold the reader spellbound with suspense.

Suddenly Nancy spotted the mysterious Arab

NANCY DREW MYSTERY STORIES

The Mystery of the 99 Steps

BY CAROLYN KEENE

NEW YORK

Grosset & Dunlap

PUBLISHERS

PRINTED IN THE UNITED STATES OF AMERICA

Contents

The Mystery of
the 99 Steps

CHAPTER I

The Strange Dream

"How exciting, Nancy! Your dad really wants Bess and me to go to France with you?" Nancy's tomboy friend exclaimed over the telephone.

"Yes, George, to help us solve a couple of mysteries. How about you girls having dinner with me tonight and I'll tell you the details."

"Give me a hint," George begged. "I can hardly wait!"

Nancy Drew laughed. "My case involves a weird dream."

"A dream!" George exclaimed. "Hypers! And what's your dad's case about?"

"Too confidential for the phone," Nancy replied. "Be here at five so we can talk it over before dinner. I'll call Bess."

Bess Marvin and George Fayne were cousins. Like Nancy, they were eighteen, and had been friends of the attractive, titian-haired girl detec-

1

tive for a long time. They arrived promptly. Blond Bess's warm smile revealed two dimples. George, with close-cropped dark hair, was slim and athletic—the exact opposite of her slightly plump cousin.

"We both have permission to go to France, Nancy," said Bess, "but please, *please* don't get me into any scary situations the way you have in your other mysteries."

Nancy grinned and put an arm affectionately around Bess. "I can't promise, but—"

"Of course you can't," George interrupted. "Besides, that's what makes solving mysteries so exciting. Now tell us all about everything."

The three girls went into the living room, where a cheerful blaze crackled in the fireplace. This was an unseasonably cool June day. Bess and George seated themselves in comfortable chairs, but Nancy remained standing, her back to the fire. Her blue eyes glistened excitedly.

"Begin!" George urged. "From your expression I'd say we shouldn't waste a minute getting these mysteries solved."

"How'd you guess?" said Nancy. "Dad has already gone to Paris on his case. We're to meet him at a hotel there and after a couple of days in Paris we girls will go for a visit to a large chateau in the country."

Bess's face glowed. "A real chateau! Divine!"

"Not only that," Nancy went on, smiling,

"we're having dinner guests tonight—they live in the chateau."

"We'll be staying with them?" Bess asked.

"No, they're visiting in the States for a few weeks and staying right in this house. You girls and I will be exchange guests."

George chuckled. "Will I be in exchange for a boy?"

Laughingly Nancy replied, "They're girls—Marie and Monique Bardot." She explained that arrangements had been made between her father and an aunt of the Bardot sisters. Carson Drew was a prominent attorney, who often was called upon to handle difficult cases. Frequently his daughter helped him.

"The girls' aunt, who is a few years older than their mother," Nancy continued, "lives here in River Heights. Marie and Monique are with her right now. But her apartment is too small to accommodate overnight guests. Mrs. Blair is the person with one of the mysteries—mine. She asked me to solve it."

Nancy went to stand by the fire. "You both know Mrs. Josette Blair, don't you?"

"Of course!" said Bess. "She's that lovely woman who lives in the apartment house near us. Don't tell me she's having more trouble and so soon after her husband and son were killed in that car accident. Now she has a sprained ankle! Poor Mrs. Blair," Bess added sympathetically.

"This is another kind of trouble," Nancy told the cousins. "It's weird. Every night Mrs. Blair has a horrible nightmare and wakes up with her heart pounding. In her dream she's blindfolded and is about to fall down a long flight of stairs, with someone whispering, '99 steps.'"

"How horrible!" Bess murmured.

"But," put in practical George, "at least it's only a dream. What's the mystery?"

"The mystery of the 99 steps," Nancy answered. "You see, Mrs. Blair lived in various places in France as a small child, and actually had this frightening experience, but she can't remember where or anything else about it. For years she did not think of what happened but recently had the dream again. Then something occurred that has really frightened her."

"What was it?" George asked.

Nancy said that Mrs. Blair had received a letter from Paris, written in French. "Unfortunately, in a moment of panic she destroyed the message. There was only one sentence in it. 'Tell no one about the 99 steps. Monsieur Neuf'!"

"Mr. Nine, eh?" Bess murmured, and Nancy nodded.

"It's our job," she continued, "to find Monsieur Neuf and where the 99 steps are, and—well, solve the mystery so poor Mrs. Blair can sleep peacefully again."

As Nancy stooped to poke the fire and put on

another log, Bess groaned. "I can see danger ahead with this mysterious Mr. Nine."

Suddenly the three girls were startled by a loud whirring noise. "A helicopter!" George cried out. "It's awfully close!"

The girls listened tensely, knowing it was against a River Heights ordinance for any aircraft to fly so low over the residential area. Was the pilot in trouble?

An instant later a strong downdraft of air burst from the chimney. It sent sparks, soot, and ashes over Nancy and into the room.

"Oh, Nancy!" Bess screamed.

She rushed forward with George to help Nancy. They patted out the sparks in her hair and on her sweater. Then George trampled some burning fragments on the carpet.

The scream had brought Mrs. Hannah Gruen, the Drews' housekeeper, running from the kitchen. She was a kind, pleasant-faced woman who had helped to rear Nancy since the sudden death of Mrs. Drew when the girl was three years old.

Hannah exclaimed, "What happened? Oh, my goodness!" she added, seeing Nancy covered with soot and ashes.

"That helicopter!" George exclaimed. "I'll bet it caused this mess!"

While Bess told Mrs. Gruen about the chimney episode and Nancy went upstairs to bathe, George dashed outdoors. She could see the helicopter in the distance, apparently getting ready to land at the River Heights airport.

"That pilot ought to be reported!" George thought angrily.

When Nancy came downstairs, George mentioned this and Nancy agreed. "I'll drive out to the airport tomorrow morning to see about it."

"In the meantime, Detective Drew," put in Bess, "tell us more about your mystery. For instance, how did Mr. Nine find out where Mrs. Blair is?"

"I suppose from her relatives in France. We'll ask Marie and Monique when they come. Maybe they can give us some other clues, too."

At that moment a taxi drove up and two attractive, dark-haired girls alighted. Each carried a large and a small suitcase. Nancy went to the door to meet them.

"You are Nancy Drew?" asked the taller of the pair, smiling. She had a musical voice with a delightful accent.

Nancy smiled. "*Oui.* And you are Marie, *n'est-ce pas?*" She turned to the shorter girl. "Hello, Monique. Please come in, and welcome!"

As soon as the Bardots were in the hall, Nancy introduced Bess, George, and Mrs. Gruen. Then the visitors' bags were carried upstairs.

"What a charming house!" exclaimed Monique when all the girls were seated in the living room. "You are very kind to invite us, Nancy.

George and Bess rushed forward to help Nancy

We do not want to be any trouble. Mrs. Gruen must give us something to do."

Conversation turned to Mrs. Josette Blair's mystery. The sisters felt sure none of the family in France had given their aunt's address to anyone. Marie and Monique were worried about the mysterious message she had received.

"Perhaps Tante Josette should go away," said Marie.

"I'm sure Mrs. Gruen would be glad to have her stay here," Nancy offered. "Perhaps she wouldn't be so frightened if she weren't alone."

"*Merci bien,*" Monique said gratefully.

Presently Hannah announced dinner. At the table the group continued to discuss the mystery of the 99 steps, but the French visitors could shed no light on the subject. Nancy did not refer to her father's case. Bess and George, though disappointed, realized that it was a confidential matter and Nancy would tell them about it later.

Nancy herself was thinking, "I'll drive Bess and George home and tell them Dad's mystery then."

A luscious-looking lemon meringue pie had just been served by Hannah Gruen when the front doorbell rang.

"I'll get it," said Nancy. "Excuse me."

At the door Nancy was startled to see a man wearing a half mask! "This is the home of the Drews?" he asked in a strong French accent.

"Y-yes," Nancy replied. Fearful he would force his way inside, she held the door firmly.

The masked man did not try to enter, and Nancy made quick mental notes of his appearance. He was tall, with exceptionally long arms and feet.

The stranger, who wore heavy leather gloves, handed Nancy a sealed envelope, turned on his heel, and left. She noted that he walked with a slight limp and wondered if this was genuine. He disappeared down the winding driveway and Nancy closed the door. The typewritten address on the envelope was to Mr. and Miss Drew.

"Why was the man wearing heavy leather gloves—in June? This could be a dangerous trick," Nancy thought, her detective instinct for caution aroused.

She carried the envelope upstairs. To be rid of any possible contamination from it, Nancy washed her hands thoroughly, then put on leather gloves.

Using a letter opener, she carefully slit the envelope. A single sheet fell out with a typed message:

STAY OUT OF FRANCE!
MONSIEUR NEUF

"Monsieur Neuf!" Nancy thought in dismay. "Was he the man who brought this?"

CHAPTER II

The Frightened Financier

At once Nancy rushed to the telephone in her father's bedroom and called Mrs. Blair. She told her of the warning note and asked if the first message from Monsieur Neuf had been typed also.

"Yes, on a French typewriter. You know many of the keys have different characters."

"Then the warning I just received was typed on another machine—an American one," Nancy said. "Monsieur Neuf probably has a confederate in this country. By the way, Mrs. Blair, we were going to suggest that you stay here with our housekeeper and your nieces while Dad and I are away."

"That's sweet of you," said Mrs. Blair. "Let me think it over. It's you I'm worried about— not myself. I don't want you to take any undue risks for me."

Nancy replied in as lighthearted a tone as she could muster, "Oh, don't worry, Mrs. Blair, I must take risks when solving a mystery."

Some traps and scary situations in which she had found herself flashed through the young detective's mind, from her very first mystery involving *The Secret of the Old Clock* to her recent adventure—capturing *The Phantom of Pine Hill*.

"I'm sure you do take risks," Mrs. Blair said. "But I beg of you, be careful."

When Nancy returned to the dining room, she told the others about the masked man who had left the warning note. Everyone looked worried.

"Oh dear! You are in danger, Nancy, because of Monique and me," Marie burst out. "We will leave."

"No indeed you won't," Nancy replied firmly. "Monsieur Neuf is trying to keep me from going to France. But I'll go just the same. Dad wants me there. Besides, I have a job to do. I must solve your aunt's mystery. After I leave, I hope you people won't be bothered again."

Marie and Monique glanced at each other, as if unconvinced, but finally they smiled. Monique said, "Nancy, you are brave as well as kind. We will remain."

All the girls thanked Mrs. Gruen for the delicious meal, then insisted that she watch television while they cleared the table and tidied the kitchen. Shortly afterward, when Marie and

Monique excused themselves to unpack, Bess and George declared they must leave. Nancy offered to drive them home.

As soon as the three girls were on their way, George said, "Now tell us about your father's case."

Nancy chuckled. "He calls it 'The Case of the Frightened Financier.'"

Bess giggled. "Who is this money man?" she asked. "And what's he frightened about? The stock market?"

"His name is Monsieur Charles Leblanc. We don't know why he's frightened."

Bess murmured dreamily, "Frenchman. Mmm!"

Nancy went on, "He lives in a chateau in the Loire River valley, and his office and a factory he manages are in Paris. He's wealthy and influential in business circles but inherited most of his financial empire. Lately he has become very secretive—is drawing large sums of cash from banks and threatens to close up his factory."

"And put all those people out of work?" George broke in.

"Right. He has sold large holdings of stocks and bonds, too, which isn't good for the country's economy."

"Nancy, how does your dad fit into this picture?" Bess asked.

"Monsieur Leblanc's business associates have

engaged Dad to find out what has scared him into doing this. An American lawyer on vacation in France wouldn't be suspected by the 'frightened financier' of trying to learn what's going on."

As Nancy finished speaking, she pulled up in front of the Marvins' home. The girls said good night and Nancy went on to the Faynes'.

"By the way," said George, "when are we taking off?"

"Day after tomorrow. Meet you at the airport eight-thirty A.M. sharp. Good night."

During the drive home Nancy's thoughts dwelt on the mystery. On a deserted street she was suddenly startled when a man stepped off the curb directly into her path! He limped forward, then fell. Nancy jerked the steering wheel hard and jammed on her brakes to avoid hitting him. Shaken, she stared out at the prone figure.

"Help!" he cried, with a French accent. "I am sick!"

Nancy's first instinct was to assist him, but instead she reached for the door locks and snapped them. *The man on the pavement was the masked messenger who had come to her house earlier*. This must be a trick! He had followed her and knew the route she probably would take home!

Quickly Nancy pulled the car near the opposite curb and drove off. In the rear-view mirror she could see the man picking himself up and limping to the sidewalk. On a chance she had been wrong, Nancy stopped a patrol car and told her story.

"We'll investigate at once, miss," said the driver.

A little while after arriving home Nancy telephoned police headquarters and learned that the suspect had vanished. The young sleuth, convinced the man had been feigning illness, told her French friends and Hannah of the incident.

Mrs. Gruen sighed. "Thank goodness you're home safe."

Marie and Monique looked concerned, but made no comment. Nancy felt sure they were wondering if all American households were as full of excitement as this one!

The trying events were forgotten temporarily, when the visitors offered to sing duets in French. Nancy and Hannah were delighted.

"These are old madrigals from the Loire valley where we live," Monique explained. "You will hear them often while you are there."

"The songs are beautiful," Nancy said, clapping.

Mrs. Gruen applauded loudly. "This is just like having a free ticket to a lovely concert," she said, smiling.

Before the group went to bed, Nancy invited the visitors to accompany her to the airport the next day. She told them about the helicopter that had buzzed the Drew home.

The three girls arrived there in the middle of the morning. Nancy spoke to the man at the regular service counter and was directed to the office of a private helicopter company.

A young man at a desk had to be prompted twice before replying to Nancy's question. He kept staring with a smile at the two French girls.

"Oh, yes," he finally said to Nancy, "a man was up with me yesterday—the one who's going to build the helipad on your roof."

Nancy stared at the young pilot, speechless. Then she said, "You're kidding!"

"Kidding, the girl says!" He rolled his eyes around and shrugged his shoulders. "No, this is for real."

Suddenly Nancy realized the pilot had been the victim of a hoax that perhaps tied in with Monsieur Neuf. She decided to be cagey in her questioning.

"Who told *you?*" she asked.

"Why, the man I took up. Guess you know him—James Chase."

"Was he from the—er—company that's going to build the helipad on our roof?" Nancy asked.

"Yes. He showed me a letter from the A B Heliport Construction Company signed by the president. I don't remember his name. It said what they were going to do and asked if I'd fly him low over your house. I got permission to do it."

"Next time you fly low you'd better be more careful," Nancy warned. "We had a fire going and you caused a downdraft that could have set our house on fire."

"Gosh, I'm sorry about that."

"I don't know this James Chase," Nancy said. "What does he look like?"

The pilot grinned. "Queer-looking duck about fifty-five years old. Real long face and arms and feet. Limped a little."

"Anything else?" Nancy asked, her pulses quickening.

"Well, he spoke with a French accent."

Nancy thanked the pilot for his information and left with her guests. When the three were out of earshot of his office, Nancy said excitedly, "James Chase is the masked man who came to my house!"

Marie and her sister exchanged quick glances. "Nancy," Marie burst out, "we think we know who this man is. His name is not James Chase!"

CHAPTER III

The Green Lion

"You know who the masked man is?" Nancy cried out unbelievingly.

"We are not acquainted with him," Marie answered. "But I'm sure he was a gardener at the chateau of friends of ours. He was discharged for not being honest. In fact he was later suspected of stealing large sums of money from several shops."

Monique spoke up. "We remember him because he was so odd looking, although I don't recall he limped. His first name was Claude. We don't know the rest."

"And," Nancy said, "he could be Monsieur Neuf! But if Neuf is trying to keep people away from the 99 steps, why would he leave France? Girls, you've given me a very valuable clue, anyway. Since you say Claude was not honest, and he's using an assumed name and sent that warning note to Dad and me, I think our police should be alerted."

When they reached headquarters, Nancy took the Bardot sisters inside to have them meet Chief McGinnis. The middle-aged, rugged-looking officer, a good friend of the Drews, greeted them all with a warm smile.

"I'm glad to meet your French visitors, Nancy," he said.

"You'll be doubly glad," said Nancy, "when they tell you about the man who is trying to keep me from going to Paris."

After Chief McGinnis had listened to the story, he nodded gravely and turned to the Bardots. "Will you young ladies compose a cable to your friends and ask for Claude's last name and his address in France. I'll send it, but the reply will come to your house, Nancy."

The officer winked, adding, "I wouldn't want the Bardots' friends to think Marie and Monique are having trouble with the River Heights' police!"

"Oh, no, no," said Marie, and the sisters laughed.

Everyone was pleased at the quick response that came from France. The three girls, after a sightseeing trip on the Muskoka River, arrived home at five o'clock. Hannah Gruen had just taken the message over the telephone. It said:

Name Claude Aubert. Whereabouts unknown.

"Good and bad news at the same time," Nancy remarked. "Apparently Claude the gardener has disappeared from his home town. But won't *he* be surprised when our River Heights police pick him up!"

She dialed headquarters at once. Chief McGinnis was still there. Upon hearing Nancy's report, he said, "I'll get in touch with immigration authorities in Washington at once to check if Aubert entered this country legally. Most offices will be closing, but I'll call anyhow." He paused. "My men are out looking for this Frenchman. When do you leave, Nancy?"

"At eight tomorrow morning."

"Well, if I have any news before then I'll let you know. Good-by now."

"Good-by, and thanks!"

Monique turned to Nancy. "Oh, I hope the police catch Claude! He may try to harm you again before you leave."

The telephone rang. Nancy answered. "Hi, Bess! What's up?"

"You must help us out—tonight."

"How?"

"By performing anything you like. Play the piano, do tricks, tell a mystery story."

"Bess, what *are* you talking about? Is this some kind of gag?"

"No, indeed, Nancy. This is the night the Teeners Club entertains the Towners Club, remember? You had to decline because of your trip."

"Sorry, Bess," said Nancy. "I'm afraid I must decline again for the same reason. I haven't finished packing yet, and I told Mrs. Blair I'd drop in to see her. She was trying to find some clues for me from old diaries of her mother's."

"But, Nancy, we need one more number. We Teeners can't disappoint the older folks. Couldn't you just—?"

"Bess," Nancy said suddenly, "I just had a brainstorm. Maybe Marie and Monique will sing some madrigals."

"Marvelous!" Bess exclaimed. "Oh, Nancy, you're a whiz. Hurry up and ask them."

At first the French girls demurred, feeling that they did not sing well enough to perform in public. When Nancy, backed by Mrs. Gruen, assured the sisters they sang beautifully, the girls consented.

Monique said happily, "Marie and I brought old-time costumes used by singers in the Loire valley. We thought Tante Josette would like to see them."

"That's great," said Nancy, hugging the girls.

When she told Bess the good news, there was a squeal of delight from the other end of the wire. "I'll pick up Marie and Monique at seven-thirty," said Bess.

Nancy requested that the sisters come last on the program. "I'll try to finish my visit with Mrs. Blair in time to hear them."

A little later when Marie and Monique came downstairs in their costumes, Nancy and Mrs. Gruen clapped in admiration. The long-skirted bouffant dresses with tight bodices were made of fine flowered silk. Marie's was blue and trimmed with narrow strips of matching velvet. Her sister's was rose color with festoons of shirred white lace.

The girls' hair was piled high on their heads and they had powdered it to look like the wigs worn by the elegant ladies of the eighteenth century. On one cheek of each singer was a tiny black patch, another custom of the day.

"You will make a great hit," Mrs. Gruen prophesied.

"*Merci beaucoup,*" said Marie, her cheeks flushed with excitement. "Mrs. Gruen, are you not going?"

"I hadn't planned to, since Nancy was not performing," the housekeeper replied.

At once the three girls urged her to attend. Hannah beamed. "All right. It won't take me long to change."

She hurried to her room and soon returned in a becoming navy-blue dress. A few moments later Bess arrived for her passengers and they left. Nancy set off in her car for Mrs. Blair's apartment.

The attractive woman, about forty years old, opened the door and said eagerly, "I found some notes in Mother's diary that may help us."

She sat down beside Nancy on a low couch in the living room and opened a small red-velvet-covered book. The writing was precise and quite faded in places.

"I've had a hard time deciphering this," said Mrs. Blair. "It tells mostly of my parents' travels, and mentions that I went along sometimes. But I was always with my governess."

"Then the experience you dream about," Nancy guessed, "could have included your governess. Is she still living in France?"

"I really don't know. To me she was just 'Mademoiselle' and that is what she's called in the diary. She was very kind, I remember. I was only three years old at the time."

Mrs. Blair gave the names of several famous chateaux they had visited. Another was where Marie and Monique lived.

Nancy's eyes sparkled. "Now we have something to work on! We'll go to each chateau and look for the 99 steps!"

"Another place mentioned in the diary, Chateau Loire, was mostly in ruins," Mrs. Blair went on. "It says the place was haunted by a ghostly alchemist who carried on his work there. You know, Nancy, in olden times people were superstitious about chemists and their experiments, and they were forbidden by law to work their 'miracles.'"

"But they did it in secret?" Nancy asked.

"Oh, yes. They had all kinds of signs, and symbols and special words to indicate to other people in their group what they had accomplished."

"How clever—and daring!" said Nancy.

Mrs. Blair arose and took a book from a shelf. It too was in French. She showed it to Nancy. "One of the interesting sets of symbols includes a Red King, White Queen, Gray Wolf, Black Crow, and Green Lion. The Red King stood for gold; the White Queen, for silver. I don't understand the meaning of the crow, but the Green Lion—he's a bad one. He devours the sun—or in other words, he's acid making the silver or gold look green."

"That's fascinating!" Nancy exclaimed.

"Yes, it is," the woman agreed. "And it's hard to realize that the forbidden art of alchemy finally became the basis for our modern chemistry. In the sixteenth century alchemists believed that minerals grew, so certain mines were closed to give the metals a chance to rest and grow."

Nancy listened intently as Mrs. Blair went on, "For a long time people laughed at this idea. But today chemists have discovered that metals do literally grow and change, though very slowly. My goodness!" the woman exclaimed. "We have wandered off the subject of our mystery, Nancy. But actually I didn't find any other clues to my dream or the 99 steps' incident of my childhood."

Nancy glanced at her wrist watch. She was reluctant to leave, but would still have time to hear Marie and Monique perform. She invited Mrs. Blair to accompany her, but the woman declined because of her sprained ankle.

Nancy arose, saying she must go. "You have given me a lot to work on, Mrs. Blair. I'll certainly be busy in France! *Au revoir,* and I hope I'll soon have good news for you."

Nancy hurried to the school auditorium where the Teeners were giving their show. She quietly slid into a rear seat in the dim light.

The Bardot sisters had just been announced and came out before the footlights. Standing with their heads close together, they began to sing. At the end of the number the applause was terrific.

As it died down, and the sisters started the second madrigal, Nancy's eyes wandered over the audience. Suddenly she caught her breath. Directly across the aisle in the center of a row sat Claude Aubert!

"I must get the police before he leaves!" Nancy thought. Quickly and unobtrusively she made her way outside.

CHAPTER IV

Backstage Scare

WHEN Nancy reached the street she looked back to see if Claude Aubert were following, but evidently he had been unaware of her presence in the auditorium. She ran to a nearby street telephone and called police headquarters.

The officer on duty promised to send two plain-clothes detectives to the school at once. Nancy said she would meet them in the lobby, and hurried back to the school. As she entered the lobby she heard enthusiastic clapping and assumed Marie and Monique had finished their act.

"Oh, I hope Claude doesn't come out here before those detectives arrive," Nancy thought worriedly. She peered inside the auditorium. He was still in his seat.

Fortunately the audience insisted upon encores. Just before the show ended, Detective Panzer and Detective Keely walked into the lobby.

Nancy quickly led them inside and pointed out their quarry. Suddenly Claude Aubert arose, pushed into the side aisle, and, without limping, hurried toward the stage.

"Come on!" Nancy urged the detectives. "He may be planning to harm the Bardots!"

The three hurried after the French ex-gardener. He went through the door that led up a short flight of stairs to the stage. To the left of the steps was an exit to the parking lot. When the pursuers reached the spot, the suspect was not in sight.

"Where did he go?" Nancy asked in dismay.

Detective Panzer yanked open the exit door and reported, "I don't see him." He and Keely dashed outside.

The next instant a scream came from somewhere backstage. Electrified, Nancy raced up the steps where a throng milled about on stage. Many persons were asking, "What happened?"

A sob could be heard above the noise. Nancy went to investigate and found Monique in hysterics. Marie was trying to comfort her.

Seeing Nancy, they cried out together, "He threatened us!"

"Claude Aubert?"

"Yes," said Monique. "He grasped my arm so hard I screamed. Then Claude said in French,

" 'If you sisters let Nancy Drew go to France, you will suffer and she will too!' "

"He *must* be Monsieur Neuf!" Marie added fearfully.

"Where did he go?" Nancy asked.

Marie pointed to the opposite side of the stage from where Nancy had entered. When Nancy reached it, she found an exit to a walk that ran behind the building to the parking lot.

Nancy was elated. Mr. Nine was trapped! The walk ran between the school and a high concrete wall. There was no way out except through the parking lot. By this time the detectives must have nabbed the suspect!

Nancy dashed along the walk to the lot and stared ahead. A large crowd was making its way to the cars and some of the automobiles had already started to move out. The detectives were not in sight. Neither was Claude Aubert.

"Oh great!" Nancy groaned in disgust. Then she took heart. "Maybe he's already been captured and is on his way to jail!"

Nevertheless, Nancy searched thoroughly among the cars, but saw neither Claude Aubert nor the detectives. She returned to the stage. By this time Monique had calmed down and was receiving congratulations with her sister from many persons for their excellent performance.

"You certainly made a hit," said Bess, coming up with George. "Just as Hannah said."

"Oh, thank you." The Bardots smiled.

George added, "Someone told us a fresh guy came up and bothered you. Who was he?"

"A Frenchman who threatened Marie and me if we let Nancy make the trip."

"Such nerve!" George exclaimed. "What's his name?"

Nancy whispered it, then brought Bess and George up to date, telling of her suspicion that Aubert was Monsieur Neuf.

"Wow!" said George. "Mr. Nine must be worried you'll solve the mystery."

In a low tone Nancy said, "We'd better go home, and I'll call headquarters to see what happened to the detectives."

They found Mrs. Gruen waiting in Nancy's convertible. After bidding good night to Bess and George, Nancy drove off. The housekeeper was astounded at the story of the threat.

"Starting tonight, I'm going to keep the burglar alarm on all the time!" she declared. "I'm glad we had it put in."

Nancy grinned. "Marie and Monique, be careful not to come home unexpectedly. You may scare Hannah."

"Just the same," said Mrs. Gruen, "I don't like this whole thing. Nancy, perhaps you ought to postpone your trip for at least a few days."

"I can't," Nancy replied. "Dad and Mrs. Blair are counting on me. Let's not worry until we find out if Claude Aubert has been captured."

As soon as she reached home Nancy telephoned the police. The suspect, she learned, had not been brought in. Furthermore, Detective Panzer and Detective Keely had neither returned nor phoned a report.

"We assume they're still tailing their man," the desk sergeant added.

Nancy hung up, her mind in a turmoil. How had Claude Aubert escaped? Where would he show up next?

"I'll bet," she thought, "that it will be right here. I'm glad the burglar alarm is on."

After a pre-bedtime snack, Mrs. Gruen and the girls went upstairs. Nancy, who had some final packing to do, was the last one to retire. Some time later she was awakened abruptly by a loud ringing.

The burglar alarm had gone off!

Instantly the young detective was out of bed and pulling on her robe and slippers. She dashed to a window and leaned out, hoping to spot the intruder. Seeing no one, Nancy sped to her father's room in the front of the house and peered below.

"Oh, they've caught him!" she exulted.

In the rays of a flashlight, the two plainclothes-men were holding a tall, long-faced man. Aubert? Just then Mrs. Gruen, Marie, and Monique rushed in.

Nancy cried out, "The detectives got the burglar! Hurry! Let's go down!"

She quickly led the way, turning on lights as she went, and flung open the front door. The detectives marched their prisoner, now limping, into the hall. Claude Aubert!

"Hello, Miss Drew," said Detective Keely. "We saw your lights go on and thought you'd like to know we got this fellow."

"Bud here and I had a wild chase," Panzer told Nancy. "We got clues to Aubert from people all over town who saw him, but we missed him every time. We figured he might come here, so Bud and I hid near your house and waited. We let him try to jimmy the window, then nabbed him redhanded."

Nancy expressed the theory that the fugitive had eluded them at the school by running in front of the stage curtains, jumping from the platform, and mingling with the crowd leaving the auditorium. The policemen agreed. "That's why we all missed him," said Detective Keely.

The prisoner was prodded into the living room. His black eyes glared malevolently at the three girls. The man's lips moved but no intelligible sounds came through them. A quick search of his pockets by Keely revealed no passport or other identification.

As soon as Mrs. Gruen and the girls were

seated, Detective Panzer ordered, "Okay, Aubert. Talk! Tell everything from the beginning. Why and how did you sneak into this country and under what name?"

Silence.

Nancy spoke to the detectives. "I haven't introduced my friends from France—Marie and Monique Bardot. Perhaps they can act as interpreters."

"Good idea," Detective Keely agreed.

Marie was spokesman. She relayed questions from Nancy and the police to the prisoner about the threatening letters to Mrs. Blair and the Drews; the helicopter ride; the faked illness in front of Nancy's car, and his inconsistent limping. No answers from Aubert.

Finally Detective Panzer said, "We'll go now. A night in jail may loosen this man's tongue. He'll learn he can't run around threatening people."

After the men had left, Mrs. Gruen said, "We should all be thankful that awful man is in custody. Nancy—you, Bess, and George can go to France with nothing to worry about."

Nancy merely smiled. She was not so sure! The group exchanged good nights again and retired. Soon Nancy began to dream. She kept chasing after a man who carried a large sign reading:

BEWARE M. NEUF

Then a great crowd of people in old-fashioned costumes came swarming from the ruins of a chateau. They carried large bells which they were ringing lustily.

Suddenly the dream ended. Nancy was wide awake. Bells, bells! Then she realized what was happening. The burglar alarm had gone off again!

CHAPTER V

Prowler Without Footprints

WHEN Nancy reached the top of the stairway Mrs. Gruen was there. Marie and Monique appeared a few seconds later. The group hurried down and flooded the first floor with light and turned off the alarm. No sign of a prowler.

"Let's divide up and search," Nancy suggested. "Marie and Monique, will you examine the windows? Hannah, please try the doors. I'll search for anyone hiding."

The four separated. There was tense silence as the hunt went on. Nancy looked in closets, behind draperies and furniture. She found no one.

"I guess the intruder was scared away," she thought. "At least we know he wasn't Claude Aubert!"

At that moment Marie called from the dining room, "Please come here, everybody!"

The others rushed to her side. She was pointing

to a side window which had been jimmied between the sashes and the lock broken. The intruder probably had been frightened by the burglar alarm before he had a chance to climb in.

"There will be footprints outside," Mrs. Gruen spoke up.

"We'll look," Nancy said, and went for a flashlight.

The quartet trooped outdoors to the dining-room window. A few feet away from it they stopped and Nancy beamed her light over the area.

"No footprints!" Hannah exclaimed. "If somebody tried to get in the house from here, he must have been a ghost!"

Nancy had been studying the ground. Now she pointed to a series of evenly spaced holes. "I think they were made by stilts."

"Stilts!" Monique exclaimed. "You mean the person who tried to get into your house was walking on stilts?"

"That's my guess," Nancy replied.

Mrs. Gruen gave a sigh. "It seems to me that every time we have a chance to pick up a clue, somebody outwits us."

Nancy smiled. "Stilts might be a better give-away than footprints," she said cheerfully. "I'm sure there aren't many thieves who use them."

Monique asked, "Then you think the intruder meant to steal something?"

Hannah Gruen answered. "He was either a thief or intended to harm us."

Nancy's own feeling was that the stilt walker might be linked with her mystery. She returned to the house and called the police. The sergeant at the desk was amazed to hear of the second attempted break-in.

"Two alarms in one night!" he exclaimed. "But this one sounds like some boy's prank," he commented. "Probably a town hood. I'll make an investigation and see if anybody on our list of troublemakers owns a pair of stilts. Miss Drew, perhaps you have some ideas yourself about who the person was and why he wanted to break in."

"No, I haven't," she answered, "unless there's a connection between him and Claude Aubert."

The officer whistled. "In any case, I'll speak to the chief about having a detective watch your house every night until this prowler mystery is solved."

"Thank you and I'll hunt around our place for more clues," she offered.

Again Nancy organized a search party. Marie and Monique were assigned to the house. The sisters frankly admitted they did not know what to look for.

"Oh, anything that seems odd to you," Nancy replied. "For instance, table silver missing or disturbed." Even though she felt that the intruder had not entered the house, Nancy did not want to miss an opportunity to track down the slightest piece of evidence.

She and Mrs. Gruen began searching the grounds. A single set of stilt marks came from the street, ran along the curved driveway, then turned toward the window.

"There should be two sets of marks," Nancy said. "One coming and one going."

She asked Hannah to go into the house and put on the back porch and garage lights. As soon as this was done, Nancy extinguished her flashlight and stared intently at the ground.

She noticed that the top branches of a bush near the forced window were broken. Nancy looked beyond the shrub and saw that the stilt marks went across the rear lawn toward the garage.

"I guess the man stepped over the bush," she thought.

As Nancy hastened forward to follow the marks, the housekeeper joined her. Side by side the two hurried to the double garage. The door behind Nancy's convertible had been left open. As she and Hannah approached it, they stared in astonishment. Propped against the inside of the rear window of the car was a large cardboard sign. On it, printed in green crayon, were the words:

BEWARE THE GREEN LION

"How strange!" Mrs. Gruen murmured.

"How strange!" Hannah murmured

At that moment a patrol car came up the driveway and an officer stepped out. He introduced himself as Detective Braun. "Are you Miss Nancy Drew?"

"Yes. And this is Mrs. Gruen who lives with us."

The headlights of the police car had shown up the warning sign vividly. "For Pete's sake, what's that all about?" the detective asked.

"We just found it," Nancy told him. "I think the person who tried to get into our house intended to leave the warning in some room. When he was scared away, he put it here."

"Do you know what it means?" Detective Braun asked.

"I'm not sure, but the message may have something to do with a mystery I'm trying to solve." Nancy told about the old alchemists' codes, some of which Mrs. Blair had shown her.

"One man used the Green Lion as a symbol that he had figured out how to make gold look green."

Detective Braun shook his head. "This wasn't the stunt of a kid on stilts," he said. "It's a real warning."

Mrs. Gruen nodded. "I'm afraid you're right and this means trouble for Nancy in France after all. She's leaving early tomorrow morning."

Nancy, seeing how worried the housekeeper was, tried to sound lighthearted. "Not *tomorrow* morning, Hannah dear," she said teasingly. "It's already morning! Do you realize I'll be leaving home in about four hours?"

Hannah gasped. "You're right. What a terrible night you've had—just when you need a good rest!"

Braun said he would take the sign back to headquarters and have it examined for fingerprints.

"Good night," Nancy said. "And thank you."

At eight o'clock the young sleuth was ready to leave. She and Hannah Gruen and the Bardots drove to the airport in the convertible. The housekeeper would bring the car back. Marie and Monique were sad when it came time to say good-by at the loading gate.

Marie said, "I want to see Tante Josette's mystery solved, but please don't let yourself be harmed, Nancy dear."

Monique added, "Do not spend all your time on your detective work. France is so lovely to see, and please have some fun."

"I will," Nancy promised.

She had begun to worry about Bess and George, who had not yet arrived.

But a minute later the two girls came dashing up with their parents. The cousins said quick hellos and good-bys. Then the three travelers waved adieus and walked to a four-engine craft that would take them to New York. There they would change planes.

Nancy motioned Bess to a window seat while she took one next to her on the aisle. George sat across from her. Seat belts were fastened and in a few minutes the craft taxied down the runway and took off.

As soon as the lighted "Fasten Your Seat Belt" sign was turned off and the girls unbuckled their straps, Nancy said to George, "Sit on the arm of my chair. I have something exciting to tell you and Bess."

When she finished her recital of the night's adventures, both her friends gaped unbelievingly. Then Bess said worriedly, "More trouble—now with a green lion!"

George snorted. "Sounds ridiculous to me. The alchemist who worked out that code lived hundreds of years ago. Somebody came across it just by chance and is using those words to try to scare you, Nancy."

The girl detective frowned. "What puzzles me is, where does everything fit? I have a feeling it'll be some time before I put this jigsaw together."

As she spoke, Nancy could hardly hold back a yawn and slept during most of the flight to New York. Here the girls boarded a larger plane and jetted off to Paris. After they had been cleared through customs the next morning, Mr. Drew met his daughter and her friends. The tall handsome man beamed in delight at seeing the girls.

"I've been mighty lonesome without you,

Nancy," he said. "I'll enjoy showing this beautiful city to you. Now tell me, how is your mystery coming?"

Nancy chuckled. "I have one villain in jail already." She was amused at her father's upraised eyebrows and quickly reported all that had happened.

"I can hardly believe it," the lawyer said. "Well done, Nancy. You're way ahead of me."

In lowered tones, Mr. Drew continued, "I haven't learned yet why Monsieur Leblanc is acting so strangely. Whenever I meet the man I find him very pleasant but not a hard worker, though he goes to his office regularly. He hasn't given a hint as to why he is selling his investments at such an alarming rate."

Mr. Drew remarked that he was very much interested in the warning *Beware the Green Lion*.

"Dad, I've been assuming the warning was linked with my mystery," she said, "but now I wonder if it was meant for you, too. After all, the first one from Monsieur Neuf was addressed to both of us."

"You could be right."

When the travelers reached the heart of Paris, they were intrigued by the wide boulevards with their beautiful buildings and the spectacular Eiffel Tower.

"What would you girls like to visit first?" Mr. Drew asked.

George responded at once, "Notre Dame. I want to see those ugly gargoyles."

The lawyer laughed and nodded. "Notre Dame it shall be, as soon as we have checked into our hotel on the Rue de la Paix and you girls have unpacked. I have reserved a large room for you with three beds."

In an hour the group was ready for the sight-seeing trip. Mr. Drew called a taxi and they drove directly to the street called Double D'Arcole in front of the famous old cathedral.

As they stepped from the cab, Bess exclaimed, "Oh, it's gorgeous! Goodness, look at all the carvings and statues! There must be hundreds!"

"There are," Mr. Drew agreed. "Would you girls like to climb to the top of one of the two towers? You can get a better look at some of the gargoyles and also a magnificent view of the city."

"Yes, let's," George urged.

Mr. Drew led the girls around the corner into a side street with several sidewalk cafes opposite the north wall of the cathedral. A narrow door-way opened upon an even narrower circular stone staircase. The steps were precipitous and on one side barely had toe room.

"I hope we don't meet anyone coming down," Bess remarked, frowning.

Nancy went first, with Bess directly behind her. George came next and Mr. Drew brought up the rear. The stairway was rather dark in spots where light could not filter through the tiny square openings in the outer wall.

Nancy was silently counting the steps. "I may as well begin my sleuthing and see if there are any clues on the 99th step," she thought.

Slowly she and the others spiraled their way upward. Nancy had just passed the 99th step, without having seen anything significant, when she started around a sharp turn. Coming down toward her was an enormously fat woman, who blocked the entire width of the staircase.

Without regard for those below her, she descended swiftly and thoughtlessly, not moving sideways to give Nancy any room. Dismayed, Nancy stood on her toes and tried to hug the wall which was too flat to give any handhold.

"S'il vous plaît—" Nancy began.

The fat woman paid no attention. She pushed against Nancy so hard that the girl lost her balance! She fell against Bess, who in turn dropped backward onto George. Unable to keep her balance, George desperately clawed the air!

Would they all go tumbling to the bottom?

CHAPTER VI

Double Take

As the three girls tumbled down the circular stairway, Mr. Drew braced himself to try stopping them. He held one hand firmly against the inner wall and leaned forward. As the impact came he teetered, but only momentarily. The girls, too, had pressed against the stone side and this had helped to break the fall.

"Oh, thank you!" Bess cried out. "I was never so scared in my life!"

She, George, and Nancy regained their balance. The fat woman who had caused the accident had paused for only an instant. With a curt *pardon* she went on down the stairway.

The Americans laughed off the incident, but all of them sincerely hoped they would not meet any more overweight persons on the steps!

"How much farther to the top?" Bess asked, puffing a little.

Mr. Drew said that the Notre Dame tower was 226 feet high. "You should be glad you're not going to the tip of the spire," he said with a chuckle. "That's 296 feet from the ground."

"It's a tremendous building, isn't it?" Nancy remarked.

Mr. Drew nodded. "And some outstanding historical events have taken place here, including two coronations of enormous pomp and ceremony—for Henry V of England and Napoleon I."

By this time Nancy had reached the top step and walked out onto the platform of the tower with its shoulder-high stone railing. A few feet ahead of her a massive stone gargoyle protruded from the roof. It looked like some strange prehistoric bird overlooking the swift-flowing River Seine below.

As Bess reached Nancy's side, she commented, "This gargoyle and the others I can see around this tower are so ugly they're almost handsome!"

George turned to Mr. Drew. "Who ever thought up gargoyles and what does the name mean?"

"I understand," Mr. Drew replied, "that these figures are really rainspouts. Gargoyle is derived from a medieval French word meaning gurgle or gargle. As to why they were made to look so grotesque, it's thought this was a whim of the designer and the architects."

Mr. Drew and the girls walked from one end

of the platform to the other viewing as much of Paris as they could. The thing they noticed particularly was that practically all the buildings except churches had flat roofs.

"They were also in vogue in our country around the turn of the century," said Mr. Drew, "but we went back to the gabled variety. Now the flat ones are becoming popular again for large buildings. Give you one guess why."

"So helicopters can land on them," Nancy replied. Smiling, she said, "Dad, will we have to change our roof for the helipad?"

George chuckled. "Paris is ready for the future. A helipad on every roof! And the Drews won't be far behind!"

Nancy glanced down at the street from which they had entered the tower. Suddenly she grabbed her father's arm.

"Dad! That man down there! He looks like Claude Aubert!"

Mr. Drew was surprised and Bess and George dashed to Nancy's side. The man on the street was gazing upward directly at the group.

"But you said Claude Aubert was in the River Heights' jail!" Mr. Drew exclaimed.

At that moment the man apparently sensed that they were looking at him. He turned on his heel and walked away quickly.

"He's not limping!" Bess exclaimed.

As George gazed after him, she said, "Hard to

believe he escaped from jail and got over here so fast!"

Nancy remained silent, but her father spoke up. "It's possible Aubert had someone put up bail money for him, then he jumped bail and managed to catch an overseas plane somewhere."

When Nancy still did not put forth an opinion, Mr. Drew asked, "What's your theory?"

"Rather startling," she replied, "but I have a hunch this man is Claude Aubert's brother, perhaps an identical twin."

"Then which one," said George, "is the real Monsieur Neuf?"

Nancy frowned. "I don't know, but I believe they're working together—Claude in the United States, this man over here. It's my guess we've been followed ever since we arrived."

A frightened look came over Bess's face. "Then we didn't leave the danger behind. Nancy, supposing the men are brothers, do you think one calls himself the Green Lion?"

"Possibly. In any case, we should find out at once if Claude Aubert did escape, or jump bail. I'll phone Chief McGinnis as soon as we leave here."

Mr. Drew liked the idea and the four left the tower immediately. When they reached the street, Nancy suggested that Bess and George go inside the cathedral while she and her father looked for a telephone.

"There's a delightful little garden in back of Notre Dame," said Mr. Drew. "Suppose we all meet there in half an hour."

The group separated. Nancy and her father found a restaurant which had a telephone booth and Nancy put in a call to River Heights. She was told there would be a delay of fifteen minutes.

"I'll wait," she said in French. "Will you please ring me at this number?"

The operator promised to do so. Nancy and her father sat down at a nearby table and ordered some French pastry and hot chocolate. When the food arrived, Mr. Drew chuckled and said, "Wouldn't Bess be goggle-eyed over this pastry?" Nancy grinned.

Ten minutes later the telephone rang and she jumped to answer it. "Chief McGinnis?"

"Yes. You're calling from Paris, Nancy?" he said. "It must be important."

"It is. Tell me, is Claude Aubert still in jail?"

"Sure. Why?"

Quickly Nancy told him about the man she had seen. "Could you find out from Aubert if he has a brother who looks like him, perhaps a twin?"

"Hold on!" The chief was gone for several minutes.

Finally McGinnis came back and said that Aubert had refused to answer. "That makes me think you may have guessed correctly," the officer told Nancy. "By the way, we've observed that his limp is phony. Anyhow, I will report your suspicions to the Paris police."

Nancy told the chief where she was staying and thanked him for his help. She asked about the stilt walker. The man had not been found yet.

As Nancy emerged from the booth and rejoined her father, she was beaming.

"Don't tell me," said Mr. Drew. "I know from your expression you're on the right track."

Nancy laughed. "I shouldn't wear my secrets on my face." Then she remarked softly, "If this other man is Claude Aubert's brother and is following us, we should turn the tables and follow him."

"A neat trick if you can do it," the lawyer said. "But we'll keep our eyes open."

The Drews made a tour of the breathtaking interior of Notre Dame. Nancy was awed by its vastness and the beauty of the stained-glass windows and the many statues. She paused before one of the Virgin Mary, whose lovely face looked down at arms which had once cradled an infant.

"The baby's statue was mysteriously taken away," her father explained. "Stolen apparently."

"How dreadful!" Nancy exclaimed. "And how sad!"

She and her father left the cathedral and walked down the side street to the open garden at the rear. Bess and George were waiting for them and admiring the colorful beds of zinnias and petunias. The four sat down on chairs and Nancy told the cousins of her talk with Chief McGinnis. She urged that wherever they all went, each one try to spot the man she thought was Claude's brother. A few minutes later Mr. Drew suggested that they go back to the hotel and have lunch.

"That's a grand idea," Bess spoke up. "I'm starved!"

She arose, and before heading toward the street, turned slowly in a complete circle, hoping she might see the suspect. Suddenly her eyes became riveted on a black lamppost which stood near high bushes and trees at the back of the garden. She had spied a figure crouching behind the post.

"Nancy," Bess whispered quickly, "I think I see Mr. Nine!"

CHAPTER VII

Exciting Steps

As Bess pointed toward the lamppost, the man crouching behind it seemed to realize he had been discovered. He sprang up and plunged into a mass of bushes and trees behind him.

"Let's chase him!" Nancy urged, and the whole group took off in pursuit.

George reached the other side of the shrubbery first. She cried out, "I see him! He's heading for the back street!"

When they came to the Rue du Cloître, they could see their quarry running to the south.

"We mustn't let him escape!" called Mr. Drew. "You girls go on. I can't run as fast as I used to."

Nancy soon caught up to George. But at the corner of the Quai de l'Archêveché, they were stopped by a policeman wearing a tight-fitting, dark-blue tunic suit, white gauntlets, and a high-crowned, peaked cap.

"Why are you in such a hurry?" he called out in French.

Nancy pointed down the street toward the fugitive. "He is a suspect trying to get away from us!"

The officer's eyebrows lifted. "Suspected of what?" he asked.

For a moment Nancy was stumped. What did she suspect the man of? Only of being Claude Aubert's brother. Finally she said, "He has been watching and following us. We want to find out why."

By this time Mr. Drew and Bess had reached the group. The lawyer introduced himself and the girls and showed his identification.

"I beg the pardon of the Americans," the policeman said, and waved them on.

But Nancy shook her head. "Too late. Look!"

At that moment the long-armed man was jumping into a taxi. Disappointedly his pursuers watched it drive out of sight.

The policeman said cheerfully, "If the man is following you, he will be seen again. What is his name?"

"We do not know," Nancy replied. "We think it may be Aubert. By any chance, have you ever heard of a Claude Aubert?"

The officer stared at her. "*Mais oui,* mademoiselle! Claude Aubert is a well-known forger. Some time ago he faked the signature on a large check and was nearly caught by our captain, but he got away. You mean, that man you were chasing is Claude?"

"No, he's in jail in the States," Nancy replied, then added that Captain McGinnis was going to get in touch with the Paris police. On a hunch she asked whose signature Claude Aubert had forged. The group was astounded to learn it was that of Charles Leblanc! The "frightened financier"!

Nancy and her father were elated over this clue, which might prove a strong link between his case and Nancy's.

As calmly as she could, Nancy asked the officer where Claude Aubert had lived at the time he vanished. The policeman gave her the address of an apartment house in the section of Paris known as the Left Bank.

The Drews thanked him for the information and walked back toward Notre Dame. Mr. Drew suggested they have lunch at one of the sidewalk cafes instead of returning to the hotel, then go to Aubert's apartment house.

"That would be fun," Bess said eagerly. "Some fine French food will step up my brainpower. You'd like that, wouldn't you, Nancy?"

Her friend laughed. "This mystery is becoming so complicated, I can use all the help you can give me."

Mr. Drew selected a pleasant cafe and the group seated themselves at a small table. After their luncheon orders of cheese soufflé had been given, the lawyer said in a low tone, "Monsieur Leblanc's office building is not far from Aubert's apartment."

George asked, "Do you think that fact has a bearing on your case, Mr. Drew?"

The lawyer shrugged. "At least it's a strange coincidence."

When they finished eating, Mr. Drew suggested that on their way to the Left Bank, they stop at the famous Louvre to view some of the paintings and statuary. A taxi took them to the massive museum which had once been a palace.

Bess sighed. "It would take us a week to see everything in this place," she commented.

Mr. Drew smiled. "You're right, Bess, but there are certain priceless art objects you must not miss —for instance, the Winged Victory."

George grinned. "She's the lady with the wings but no head, isn't she?"

"That's the one," Mr. Drew answered.

"The Venus de Milo statue is here too," Nancy said.

"That's right."

George chuckled. "She's the beautiful lady without any arms. Where did she lose them?"

"I haven't heard," the lawyer said with a grin, "or I might look for them."

Bess announced, "One thing I want to see is Leonardo da Vinci's portrait of Mona Lisa."

Mr. Drew said that apparently this was considered the most valuable art treasure in the Louvre, since it was more heavily protected than any of the other pieces.

When the group reached the famous painting, they found it guarded by an iron rail and two uniformed men, who carefully watched each visitor.

"Mona Lisa's face is lovely," Nancy remarked. "Just looking at her portrait gives me a peaceful feeling."

The River Heights visitors stayed for an hour in the famous old building. Then, weary, they decided to stop walking and drive across the Seine to Claude Aubert's former home. The concierge in charge of the apartment house was a rather gruff man of about fifty. At first he seemed unwilling to answer any of their questions about the forger.

"It was bad enough having the police come here disturbing me!" he complained, growing red in the face. "Who are you?"

Nancy smiled disarmingly. She decided to shoot a direct question at him. Could she get him to answer?

"What's Claude Aubert's twin's name?" she asked.

Without hesitation, the concierge replied, "Louis."

Nancy could hardly keep from shouting her

delight. Mr. Drew, Bess, and George also found it difficult to maintain calm expressions.

"Oh, yes," Nancy said nonchalantly. "Let me see, where does Louis live?"

The man did not answer at once, but finally he said, "It is out in the country. I do not know the name of the place." Suddenly he went on, "You know, Louis is the bright one. Claude is a bit slow. He just does what his brother tells him to."

Mr. Drew put in casually, "Louis keeps busy, no doubt. We saw him today from a distance. What's he doing now?"

"Oh, he is some sort of scientist. That business with formulas and flasks and such is beyond me."

Nancy's intuition told her they were getting nearer and nearer to an excellent clue. Again she smiled at the concierge. "Would it be possible for us to see where Claude used to live?"

Actually Nancy did not expect to find any clue in the apartment. What she did want to do was count the number of steps to Aubert's living quarters. It was just possible there might be 99 and there would be some significance to this!

"I can show you which apartment it is," the concierge replied. "But I cannot admit you because a young man and his wife occupy it now."

As he led the way up the stairs, Nancy moved backward to the front door. Then, as she walked forward again, she began to count. It took her ten steps to the stairway. She added each tread as the group climbed. On the second floor there were ten steps to the next stairway. The concierge went on up, and Nancy continued to count. When they reached the top, she found there were 69 steps in the two stairways.

"Maybe—just maybe—" Nancy told herself.

Would there be ten steps to the Aubert apartment? There were. The total was 99!

"But now that I have the information, how can I use it?" Nancy thought. "The number may have been a signal between Louis and Claude or between Claude and some pals of his to meet here in connection with his forgeries. But where does it fit in with Mrs. Blair's dream?"

Meanwhile, the Drews and their companions had pretended to gaze with interest at the apartment door, then returned to the front entrance. Mr. Drew thanked the concierge, hailed a taxi, and the callers went back to their hotel.

"I have a surprise for you girls this evening," said Mr. Drew. "We're invited to a soirée. It's being held by friends of mine especially for you girls to meet Monsieur Charles Leblanc and see what you can learn."

"It sounds wonderful!" Bess remarked.

The lawyer turned to his daughter and smiled. "If you can get as much information from Monsieur Leblanc as you did from the policeman and the concierge, I'll buy you a special gift from Paris!"

Nancy laughed. "I'll do my best to win it!"

After tea and a short rest, Mr. Drew and the girls dressed in evening clothes and taxied to a beautiful mansion near the Bois de Boulogne Park. The large stone building had several steps leading up to a massive carved doorway. The house was brilliantly lighted, and strains of music from inside floated to the ears of the arriving guests.

"How divine!" Bess murmured.

Mr. Drew alighted first. He was just helping Nancy out when a car came up behind their taxi, and without braking, smashed into it. Despite her father's efforts to save Nancy, she was knocked off-balance and thrown full force to the pavement!

CHAPTER VIII

Dancing Sleuths

THE impact snapped Bess and George against the rear seat of the taxi, then bounced them onto the floor. The driver was also jolted, although less severely.

A stream of furious French issued from his lips and he scrambled out, shaking his fist. But the car responsible for the crash had quickly backed up, then roared off down the street before anyone could get the license number.

By this time Mr. Drew had gently helped Nancy to her feet and the taximan assisted Bess and George from the car. Although badly shaken, the cousins' first concern was for Nancy.

"Are you hurt?" they asked.

At first she did not answer. The breath had been knocked from her and she had fallen heavily on one shoulder. Nancy admitted it hurt.

"Nothing's broken, though. I'll be all right. How about you girls?"

"Okay," George said gamely, rubbing the back of her neck. "We're lucky."

Mr. Drew was greatly concerned for his daughter and her friends. "We'd better give up the party and go back to our hotel."

"Oh, no!" Nancy insisted. "I just wish we'd seen the person who crashed into us. It was certainly deliberate!"

Grim-faced, her father agreed. No one had caught even a glimpse of the culprit. Mr. Drew paid their fare and the banged-up taxi rattled off.

The door of the mansion had opened and the doorman, who evidently had heard the crash, came hurrying down the steps. Upon learning that Mr. Drew and the girls had an invitation to the soirée, he said quickly:

"I will take you to bedrooms so that you can refresh yourselves." When he saw Nancy rubbing one shoulder, he told her there was a doctor at the party. "I will send him upstairs."

Nancy protested, but the doorman was insistent. "I know Monsieur Tremaine—your host —would want me to do that."

He escorted the American guests to elegantly furnished bedrooms on the second floor. Heavily carved furniture was set off by velvet flower-patterned rugs and large tapestries which hung on the walls. The one in the girls' room showed a hunting scene with women seated sidesaddle on their horses. The costumes made the girls smile.

The women wore bodiced dresses with long skirts and large hats with plumes.

"I wonder if those women ever really did any riding or whether they just sat on the horses and posed," Bess remarked.

A few moments later the doorman brought in the physician and introduced him. He was very gracious and seemed glad that Nancy and the others spoke French, since he said he spoke little English. He examined her shoulder thoroughly and reported that it was neither broken nor strained.

"But you have a bad bruise. I suggest that an ice pack be put on it at once and that you get some rest."

Then the doctor examined Bess and George. He seemed pleased that their injuries were minor and prescribed ice packs for the bruises.

Mr. Drew summoned a maid, who quickly brought some ice. The girls lost no time in applying it.

Presently Nancy declared, "I feel all right now. Let's go down to the party."

Bess helped her put on fresh make-up and combed her hair. George brushed the dirt off Nancy's dress and used some water to remove a couple of spots.

"Thanks a million, girls," she said. "All set?"

With a smile Mr. Drew gave Nancy his arm and they led the way downstairs. News of the accident had spread among the guests and many had gathered in the reception room to meet the newcomers. Beyond, the girls could see a ballroom gleaming with crystal chandeliers.

Monsieur and Madame Tremaine were very solicitous, but Nancy and the cousins assured them they felt fine. "We are grateful to you for inviting us to the soirée," Nancy added, not revealing she knew why the party was being given.

"I should like to introduce you to some of our other guests," Madame Tremaine said.

After she had presented them to various friends, she escorted the four Americans into the ballroom where Monsieur Leblanc was standing, and introduced them. A tall slender man with iron-gray hair and mustache, he spoke English fluently.

Nancy thought, "He is handsome and has a charming smile."

"Mr. Drew," said the financier, "you are fortunate to have such a lovely daughter." His eyes beamed with admiration as he looked at Nancy. Then, turning, he smiled at Bess and George.

"Ah! We Frenchmen pride ourselves on the good-looking women in this country, Mr. Drew, but if Mesdemoiselles Drew, Fayne, and Marvin are examples of the young women in America, perhaps our women have to take second place, *non?*"

Nancy, Bess, and George as well as Mr. Drew

carried on the banter. Then Nancy adroitly brought the conversation around to another subject with the question, "You are alone this evening, Monsieur Leblanc?"

"Unfortunately, yes," he replied. "Madame Leblanc is at our house in the country. She did not feel well enough to attend."

"I'm so sorry," said Nancy. "I would have liked to meet her."

She had the feeling he might have invited the group to do so, but at that moment they were interrupted by an announcement from the leader of a small string orchestra. He introduced a young woman soprano who had just joined the Paris Opera Company. The listeners were spellbound by her clear silvery voice, and after she had finished two solos, the applause was thunderous.

Directly afterward, Monsieur Leblanc murmured *"Pardon"* to the girls and Mr. Drew, and went off. The young opera singer graciously gave an encore, then said she must leave.

As the orchestra resumed playing, Nancy, Bess, and George began to talk in subdued tones to Mr. Drew about Monsieur Leblanc. "He seemed attentive to the music," Nancy remarked, "but I did notice that once in a while during the singing he had a faraway look in his eyes."

Bess said dramatically, "Maybe he's been hypnotized and is being coerced into selling his securities!"

64 THE MYSTERY OF THE 99 STEPS

"At any rate," George declared emphatically, "I have a hunch it won't be easy to get information out of him!"

Mr. Drew nodded. "I've already learned that. But I really think you girls may have better luck."

Some of the guests they had already met began introducing the River Heights group to others. Two debonair young men asked Bess and George to dance. Another young man was just making his way toward Nancy when Monsieur Leblanc returned.

Bowing low, he said, "May I have the pleasure?"

Nancy did not want to dance—her shoulder was aching—but she felt she should not miss this opportunity to talk with the financier. As they circled the floor of the ballroom, he began to query her about her trip to France. Instantly she wondered if he suspected something, but if he did, Leblanc gave no evidence of it.

She said, "Whenever Dad's away from home he misses me very much. My mother died when I was a child and he and I have always been close pals. He asked me to join him here. Bess and George often go on trips with me."

"I wish," Leblanc said, "that I might have the honor of showing you and your friends around. But I am very busy and unfortunately have little time to myself."

When the music stopped, the Frenchman escorted Nancy to a chair, then excused himself. A few minutes later George made her way to Nancy's side, saying:

"I have something terribly important to tell you. I told my partner I'd be back in a few minutes. See that man in Arabian dress standing in the doorway?"

When Nancy nodded, George went on, "Well, what do you think of this? After Monsieur Leblanc left you, I heard him say to the Arab—in the doorway to the palm garden, where I was— 'I told you not to come here, or anywhere else, unless we were alone!' "

Nancy sat straight. "Go on!" she urged.

"The Arab replied, 'But 9 is coming up. You must meet me.' "

"This is exciting!" Nancy remarked. "What else happened?"

"Monsieur Leblanc answered, 'Tomorrow— 99.' Then the men separated."

"Ninety-nine!" Nancy echoed softly, her eyes lighting up. "I'd like to follow the Arab!"

At that moment Mr. Drew walked over and Nancy repeated what George had told her. He too was extremely interested, but said he would not permit Nancy to do any more sleuthing that evening.

"Don't forget you were banged up a while ago.

You must get back to the hotel and go to bed. I'll make a bargain with you, though. Tomorrow we'll follow Monsieur Leblanc."

"All right, Dad. Now, may I make a bargain with you?"

He smiled. "What is it?"

"I'd like to shadow the Arab here just for a few minutes and see what I can find out. Please!"

Mr. Drew agreed to give his daughter twenty minutes. "Be very careful," he warned her. "We don't want anyone becoming suspicious."

Just then a young man, Henri Durant, came up and asked Nancy to dance. She accepted and as the music started he led her onto the floor. The young sleuth glanced about as casually as possible. Suddenly her gaze fixed on the far end of the ballroom which opened onto the indoor garden with palm trees and exotic plants. She spotted the Arab in the garden!

An idea quickly came to Nancy. "I hope it works!" she thought.

As they moved along to a lively tune, Henri complimented Nancy not only on her dancing but also on her ability to speak French so well.

Nancy laughed. "You dance very well yourself." Then, seconds later, she said, "Would you mind going into the garden and sitting out the rest of this dance? My shoulder is aching."

Henri was most solicitous and at once led her to a bench in the heavy foliaged garden. At first she could not see the Arab. Then suddenly she spotted him among the palms. He was staring intently at her!

Did he know who Nancy was? Had he guessed that she was trying to solve the mystery of the 99 steps? Was this man a new enemy of hers?

Turning to her companion, Nancy asked, "Do you know who that Arab is?"

"No, but I'll be glad to find out," Henri answered.

He arose and started toward the man. But instantly the stranger turned and hurried off to the far end of the garden where there was another entrance into the ballroom.

Nancy caught up to Henri, thinking, "That Arab certainly acts suspiciously. I mustn't let him get away without finding out who he is!" Smiling, Nancy said to Henri, "I want to speak to that Arabian man and I thought he might be leaving."

This seemed to satisfy Henri and he accompanied her to the edge of the dance floor. Nancy caught sight of the Arab's turban as he disappeared out the doorway which led to the hall. She and Henri made their way through the crowd of dancers as fast as they could.

By the time they reached the hall, however, the Arab was going out the front door. Apparently he had not bothered to say good night to the Tremaines. Hurrying to the doorman, Nancy asked him who the stranger was.

"I do not know the gentleman," he replied. "He had a proper invitation, so of course I admitted him."

"I must speak to Monsieur!" said Nancy, and the servant opened the door.

She ran outside and from the top of the long flight of steps gazed up and down. The Arab was striding quickly toward a small, dark car parked up the street. There was a driver at the wheel and the motor was running.

"Come on, Henri!" Nancy urged.

CHAPTER IX

Startling Headlines

TOGETHER, Nancy and Henri dashed down the steps of the Tremaine mansion. By this time the mysterious Arab had jumped into the automobile. The driver pulled away and the car shot forward.

Suddenly, in the glare of two street lamps in front of the Tremaine home, the Arab took off his turban. With it came a wig and false whiskers.

"Oh!" Nancy gasped.

The man was Louis Aubert!

"Is something the matter?" Henri asked.

"That man was in disguise. I have an idea he had no right to be at the party. We should tell the Tremaines."

"Do you think he is a thief?" Henri looked perplexed. "Is that why you wished to stop him?"

Nancy hesitated, then answered truthfully, "I'm not sure. But I do have reason to suspect that the man is dishonest."

Henri accepted her reply as if sensing Nancy did not wish to divulge anything else. The couple re-entered the house.

Monsieur and Madame Tremaine were at the back of the hall saying good night to several guests. Nancy waited until they had departed, then asked her host who the Arab was. He and his wife

exchanged glances, then Monsieur Tremaine responded:

"We did not catch his name. He suddenly appeared and told us he was a friend of Monsieur Leblanc's. Do you wish me to ask him?"

"He has already left," Nancy told them. "He seemed to be in a great hurry."

The Tremaines frowned. Obviously the man had displayed very bad manners! Nancy was saved from explaining the reason for her query because Bess, George, and Mr. Drew joined them. The lawyer said he thought they should leave now.

Henri smiled at Nancy and said good night. Monsieur Leblanc then came up to the group. His manner seemed perfectly natural as he expressed the hope of seeing them all again some time in the near future.

Nancy's brain was in a whirl. She wondered if the financier might be staying in town and planning to meet Louis Aubert early in the morning. Smiling, Nancy asked Leblanc, "Will you go way out to the country tonight?"

"Yes, indeed. I love it there. I sleep much better."

George had caught on to Nancy's line of questioning. She spoke up. "Do you commute to your office every day, Monsieur Leblanc?"

"Yes. I will be at my desk by nine o'clock tomorrow morning, as usual," he replied.

Nancy had come to a conclusion. He would meet Louis Aubert either in Paris during the daytime or out in the country the next evening. "I can't wait to follow him," she thought.

The girls went for their wraps, and after thanking the Tremaines for a delightful evening, left with Mr. Drew. Nancy, although bursting with her news, decided not to tell it until they were alone at the hotel. Once there, she asked her father to come to the girls' room.

Nancy told about the Arab being Louis Aubert and added her suspicion that the invitation might have been obtained fraudulently.

"It could even have been forged," she said. "Remember, his brother Claude is a wanted forger. Louis could be one, too."

George in turn repeated the conversation she had overheard between Louis and Leblanc.

"These are excellent clues!" the lawyer exclaimed. "They may tie in with something I heard this evening from Monsieur Tremaine. He is one of the people who is greatly alarmed about Monsieur Leblanc's irresponsibility in business affairs."

Nancy asked eagerly, "Can you tell us why?"

"Oh, yes. Today Leblanc received a very large sum of money—thousands of dollars in francs— for the sale of certain securities. He had insisted upon having it in cash. I assume that he had the sum with him tonight."

Bess's eyes grew wide with excitement. "You mean that perhaps the poor man is being black-mailed by Louis Aubert?"

The lawyer smiled wryly. "I'm not making any definite statement yet, but what we've heard and seen tonight seems to add up to some kind of secret dealing."

He and the girls continued to discuss every angle of the mystery for nearly an hour. In the end, all agreed that the whole thing remained very puzzling.

"I still can't fit Mrs. Blair's strange dream into the picture," Nancy remarked, "yet I'm sure there's a connection."

One by one the foursome began to yawn. Mr. Drew stood up and said he was going to bed. "I'll see you all at breakfast," he added, then kissed each girl good night.

As Nancy undressed she looked woefully at her bruised shoulder. There was a large black-and-blue area. Bess asked if she wanted more ice, but Nancy shook her head.

"The doctor said I was all right and I think a good night's sleep will help a lot."

In the morning her shoulder did feel better, although it was very sensitive to the touch. Nancy smiled. "Just a little souvenir of Paris."

When the girls joined Mr. Drew in the hotel dining room, they found him reading the morning paper. As he laid it down, a headline caught Nancy's eye and she gasped.

"Monsieur Leblanc robbed on the way home!" she repeated. "And of thousands of dollars! It must have been the money he received from the securities!"

Her father nodded. "I'm afraid so."

"Have you read the whole article?" George asked Mr. Drew.

"Yes. Leblanc's car was waylaid by two men on a lonely stretch of road not far from his home. The bandits did not harm Leblanc or his chauffeur, but they did take every penny which both carried."

"How dreadful!" Bess exclaimed. "Have the thieves been caught yet?"

Mr. Drew said No, and there was probably little chance the police could do so. After the holdup, there had been rain and any footprints had been washed away.

"Mr. Drew," Bess asked, "could one of the holdup men have been Louis Aubert?"

"I confess I'm baffled," Nancy's father replied. "If that make-believe Arab is blackmailing Leblanc and was going to meet him today, why would he rob him last night? On the other hand, he may have feared Leblanc would change his mind so he decided to get the money right away."

Nancy spoke up. "One thing we haven't followed up about Louis is his being a scientist. My hunch is he's a chemist."

Bess sighed. "It's going to be hard to find out about his work if nobody knows or will tell where Aubert lives. I'll bet if Monsieur Leblanc has the address he isn't going to reveal it."

The others agreed and felt that pursuing this lead would have to wait. Nancy said, "I'd like to find out if Monsieur Leblanc plans to stay home because of the robbery."

"Why don't you call up and find out?" Bess suggested. "You can act terribly upset and sympathetic over what happened."

"I'll do that," Nancy said. "I'll phone his office."

Shortly after nine, Nancy put in the call. She learned from the operator that Monsieur Leblanc was there, and appeared to show no ill effects of the incident. "He is busy in a conference," the girl told her. "Would you like to leave a message?"

"No, thank you. I just wanted to make sure that Monsieur Leblanc is all right." Nancy rang off before the operator might ask who was calling.

When Mr. Drew heard his daughter's report, he decided to get in touch with Monsieur Tremaine and suggest that a private detective be retained to watch Leblanc's office building that day and follow the financier wherever he might go.

Mr. Tremaine readily agreed and asked if the detective should continue his assignment that evening also.

"Thank you, no. The girls and I will take over then."

Nancy was eager to pursue her sleuthing, but she went sightseeing with her friends and had lunch aboard a pleasure boat on the River Seine. Later, while buying some souvenirs, Nancy said, "Look! A musical coffeepot! I'll buy it for Hannah Gruen!"

Late in the afternoon Mr. Drew and the girls picked up a car he had rented earlier. They drove to Monsieur Leblanc's office building and parked nearby.

Immediately a man in street clothes walked up to them. Smiling and tipping his hat to the girls, he inquired, "Monsieur Drew? Monsieur Carson Drew?"

When Mr. Drew nodded, the man presented a card identifying him as the detective assigned to watch Leblanc.

"Monsieur Leblanc has not come out all day," the detective reported. "Do you want me to stay longer?"

"No, that won't be necessary," Mr. Drew replied. "We'll relieve you now."

Not long after the detective had left, the financier emerged from the building. He walked briskly to an automobile with a chauffeur at the wheel and got in.

A few seconds after Leblanc's car started off, Mr. Drew pulled out and followed him easily, but for only half a block. Then the dense rush-hour traffic closed in, making it impossible for Mr. Drew to keep close to their quarry. In a few moments he had lost sight of the financier's car completely.

Nancy sighed. She was very disappointed. "What if Monsieur Leblanc stops for a rendezvous at the 99 steps!" she thought. "We'll miss a perfect chance to find out where they are."

As the Drews were debating what to do next, Bess spoke up. "I'm absolutely famished. Couldn't we stop somewhere for just a quick bite—and then look for Monsieur Leblanc?"

Nancy started to agree when a sudden idea struck her. "First let's go back to Claude Aubert's old apartment!" she exclaimed.

"Why?" Bess asked.

"Monsieur Leblanc might be heading there right now—to meet Louis!"

CHAPTER X

A Sinister Figure

MR. Drew threaded his way through the Paris traffic to the Left Bank. When they reached the apartment house, the travelers scanned both sides of the street. Leblanc's car was not in sight.

"I guess he didn't come here after all," the lawyer said.

Before leaving the area, however, Mr. Drew drove around the two adjoining blocks. Still no sign of Monsieur Leblanc.

"He probably went straight home," Bess remarked. "Do we eat now?" she asked hopefully.

Mr. Drew chuckled. "Right away."

Soon he pulled up at a small cheerful restaurant which was willing to serve dinner earlier than was customary in Paris. Bess regarded the menu suspiciously.

"Snails!" she exclaimed. "And fish served whole—I just can't stand to look at the eyes of a fish on a platter!"

Mischievously Nancy pointed to another item. "Why not try this, Bess? It's very popular here—raw beef mixed with chopped onions and an uncooked egg."

Bess was horrified. "That's even worse!"

The others laughed and George said, "Why, Bess Marvin, I thought you were a gourmet!"

"Sorry," said Bess. "I'll stick to good old cream of tomato soup, medium-well-done roast beef, potatoes, asparagus, salad, some cheese, and then fruit."

George looked at her cousin disapprovingly. "You'll be bursting out of your clothes within three days if you eat like that!" As a compromise, Bess said she would not have the soup.

The food was delicious, and everyone enjoyed the meal immensely. It was seven o'clock before they left the restaurant.

"How far away does Monsieur Leblanc live?" Nancy asked her father.

"About twenty miles outside of Paris."

On the way, Nancy did not talk much. She was mulling over the various angles to the mystery. There was no doubt now but that both her case and her father's revolved around the 99 steps. Her one clue to them so far had faded out.

"If I could only unearth another clue to the right steps!" Nancy said to herself.

Mr. Drew had come to an area of handsome

homes, most of them with extensive grounds. The girls exclaimed over their attractiveness. In a little while they reached an estate which Mr. Drew said belonged to Monsieur Leblanc. It was surrounded by a high stone wall, and the entranceway was almost hidden by a grove of sycamore trees. Nancy's father pulled in among them and stopped.

"I'll hide the car here," he said. "It will be easy to take out and follow Leblanc if necessary."

"What if he doesn't come outside?" Nancy asked. "Shall we go up to the house when it's darker?"

"We'll have no choice."

They waited in the car for over fifteen minutes, then George burst out, "I need exercise! Let's do some walking!"

The others agreed and Nancy added, "We can try a little sleuthing too."

Mr. Drew locked the ignition and took the key. As the four passed through the driveway entrance, they noticed a great stone pillar on either side. Tall iron gates were attached to them, but they stood open.

"Just put here for decoration," Mr. Drew observed. "I imagine they're never closed."

Nancy suggested that the group separate. "Bess and George, suppose you take the right side of the driveway up to the house. See if you can pick up any clues as to what Monsieur Leblanc is frightened about. Dad and I will take the other side and meet you there."

Mr. Drew added, "If you two girls see Leblanc leaving, give our birdcall warning and run as fast as you can back to the car so we can follow him."

Bess and George set off among the trees that grew along the driveway. It was dark under the heavy foliage and they kept stumbling over roots.

"I wish we'd brought flashlights," Bess complained.

"We couldn't have used them, anyhow," George retorted. "Someone would spot us right away."

They went on silently for a few minutes, then Bess whispered fearfully, "I don't like this. There may be watchdogs prowling around."

"Oh, don't be silly!" said George and hurried ahead.

Suddenly Bess let out a scream. George dashed back. "What is it?"

Bess, ashen-faced, stammered out, "There! Hanging from that tree! A—a body!"

George turned a little squeamish herself, but decided to investigate. She went over, felt the object, and then laughed softly.

"It's only a stuffed dummy," she declared.

"Why is it hanging there?" asked Bess, still trembling. "It must be some kind of a sinister warning. I'm not going another step. Let's go back to the car."

"And run out on Nancy? Nothing doing," George replied firmly. "Do you know what I think this figure might be? A punching bag!"

"You mean, like football players use in practice?" Bess asked.

George nodded.

Finally Bess summoned up enough courage to go on, and presently the cousins found themselves at the head of the driveway. On the far side stood a large and imposing chateau. The girls would have to cross in the open to reach it. They discussed whether or not it was wise to do this.

The front of the mansion was well lighted. Several windows stood open, but not a sound came from inside.

"I wonder if Monsieur Leblanc is at home," George murmured.

Before she and Bess could make up their minds what to do, the front door opened. A tall, slender woman, holding a mastiff on a leash, walked down the short flight of steps. Hastily the cousins ducked back among the trees as the woman turned in their direction. Had she heard Bess's scream and was coming to investigate?

"I told you they'd have a watchdog!" Bess groaned. "We'd better go before she lets that beast loose!"

George did not argue, and the two girls began to retrace their steps hurriedly.

Meanwhile, Nancy and her father had made their way cautiously toward the rear of the big house. A little way behind it was a five-car garage, filled with automobiles. The Drews recognized the car in which Leblanc had ridden earlier.

"Dad, this must mean he's at home," Nancy said.

Directly behind the house was a large flower garden. The Drews entered it and walked along a path. Fortunately it was dark enough so that their figures could not be seen in silhouette. They passed what Mr. Drew said were the kitchen and dining room. Just beyond was a brightly lighted room with a large window, partly open, that overlooked the garden.

The room was lined with bookshelves, and comfortably furnished. In the center stood a mahogany desk. The Drews could see no one.

A moment later a telephone on the desk began to ring. The door to the room opened and a tall man strode in.

"Monsieur Leblanc!" Nancy whispered excitedly. "He *is* home! Now we can follow him if he leaves!"

Her father said, "Remember, he may already have met the man we think is Louis Aubert. Let's wait and see what happens."

Monsieur Leblanc did not lower his voice and

through an open window his part in the phone conversation came clearly to the Drews.

"I told you the money was stolen!" the financier said. "If I did not have the money, what was the use of my coming?"

Another long pause. Then Leblanc said firmly, "Now listen. People are beginning to show some suspicion. I will have to be more careful."

There followed a long silence. At last he spoke again. "It is against my better judgment. Let us not do anything more for a few days."

Nancy was hardly breathing. She did not want to lose one word that this enigmatic financier was saying.

Leblanc's voice grew angry. "Why can't you wait? I know you said 9 was coming up, but even the thought of it brought me bad luck. Every cent I had with me was taken."

The next pause was so long that Mr. Drew and Nancy began to wonder if the caller had hung up. But finally they heard Monsieur Leblanc say in a resigned tone, "Very well, then. I will go to the orange garden." He put down the telephone.

CHAPTER XI

Clue From Home

NANCY squeezed her father's arm and whispered, "The orange garden! Do you think it's here?"

Mr. Drew shook his head. "I know every inch of these grounds."

The two became silent again as they wondered where the orange garden might be and if the telephone caller had been Louis Aubert. "I'm sure he was," Nancy thought, and hoped Monsieur Leblanc would start out immediately.

The Drews watched him intently. Leblanc did not leave the study, however. Instead, he took off his jacket and slipped on a lounging robe. Then he sat down at the desk and wrote for several minutes.

"It doesn't look as if he's going out tonight," Nancy remarked.

At that moment the Frenchman picked up a book from his desk and went to a large leather easy chair. He sank into it and began to read.

"I guess this settles the matter," said Mr. Drew in a low voice. "We had better go."

His daughter lingered. "Maybe Monsieur Leblanc is going out later."

Mr. Drew smiled. "I think it's more likely he'll stop at this mysterious orange garden on his way to the office. But we can't stay here all night. Remember, you girls leave for the Bardots' chateau tomorrow."

Reluctantly Nancy started back with her father. Just then they heard a series of deep-throated barks. "That's the Leblancs' guard dog," Mr. Drew said.

"Oh!" Nancy cried out. "It may be after Bess and George! We'd better find out!"

The Drews hurried from the garden and raced quickly down the driveway. The barking continued. When Nancy and her father reached the entrance, the gates were locked.

There was no escape!

"This is bad!" Mr. Drew exclaimed. "Nancy, I'll boost you to the top of the wall. The dog won't harm you there."

"But how about you?" Nancy argued. "And where are Bess and George?"

At that moment the cousins appeared, running like mad. The mastiff's barks were closer now.

"Quick! Over the wall!" Nancy said. "The gates are locked!"

Bess and George did not say a word. Quickly

Mr. Drew helped them to the top of the stone-work, then he boosted Nancy upward. She and George lay flat on the wall and grasped the law-yer's hands. The dog, his leash trailing, had reached the scene and managed to tear one cuff of Mr. Drew's trousers before the girls yanked him to safety.

Out of breath the group dropped to the ground and went to their car. As they headed for Paris, Mr. Drew remarked, "I guess we got what we deserved. We *were* trespassing."

Bess said, "Thank goodness we escaped. Two scares in one night are two too many for me."

She and George told the story of the figure hanging from a tree. When Mr. Drew heard George's idea that the dummy was a punching bag for Monsieur Leblanc, he laughed heartily. "I've been calling him the frightened financier, but maybe I'll have to change it to the fighting financier!"

The girls giggled, then George eagerly asked what Nancy and her father had found out. When they were told about the orange garden, the cousins agreed it was an excellent clue.

"How are you going to follow it up, Nancy?" Bess queried.

"Right now I don't know. But I intend to find out where the orange garden is."

Nancy went on to say that one thing was very puzzling: Why did Louis Aubert have such a hold over Monsieur Leblanc, when his name had once been forged by Aubert's twin, Claude?

Her father said this mystified him too. "I'm afraid we'll have to wait for the answer to that question, Nancy, until you turn up more evidence about the exact relationship between Louis and Monsieur Leblanc."

Next morning, when the girls came downstairs to breakfast, Mr. Drew said, "I've rented a car for your trip to the Loire valley, girls."

"Wonderful! Thank you, Dad," said Nancy. "You think of everything."

The lawyer smiled. "I have another surprise for you." He pulled a letter from his pocket. "Some news from Hannah Gruen."

Nancy excused herself and read the letter. Marie and Monique were having a good time in River Heights. The sisters were popular and they had made some warm friends. There were two special messages for Nancy. One was from Chief McGinnis. The River Heights police had caught the stilt walker! He had been paid, he said, by a James Chase to do the job.

"Claude Aubert again!" Nancy murmured, then quickly told the others about the stilt walker's arrest. She read on. Suddenly she said excitedly, "Oh, listen to this, everyone!

" 'Here's the other special message for you, Nancy. Right after you left, Mrs. Blair phoned to say she'd had the dream about the 99 steps, as usual. But this time she was a child, playing with her governess. Presently the woman tied a dark handkerchief over the child's eyes for a game of blindman's buff. Later, Mrs. Blair came across another clue in her mother's diary—the name of the governess. It was Mlle. Lucille Manon.' "

Nancy looked up from the letter and burst out, "How's that for a marvelous clue?" Mr. Drew, Bess, and George were elated by the information.

The girls had packed before leaving their room, so soon after breakfast they checked out of the hotel and were on their way to the Bardots. Nancy, at the wheel of the small French car, found it took some time to make progress. The morning rush hour was in full swing, with its hurrying crowds and hundreds of taxis scooting recklessly in and out of traffic.

The route to the Bardots led past the famous palace of Versailles. Nancy paused briefly so that the girls could view the huge building and gardens.

"Let's see," Bess mused, "wasn't it Louis XIV who built Versailles?"

Nancy nodded. "It has a fascinating history. Imagine a German emperor being crowned here! You remember that Germany once controlled all of France."

"But the French finally got their country back," George remarked.

Suddenly Bess chuckled. "The thing I remember is that Louis XIV was supposed to have had over a hundred wigs. He never permitted anybody to see him without one, except his hairdresser."

Presently the girls came to the Bardots' home. Set far back from the street, it was approached by a curving driveway. The stone dwelling was in the style of an old French period when buildings were square and three stories high. It had a flat roof with a cupola for a lookout.

"Isn't it lovely here?" Bess remarked as she looked around at the green lawns, the well-trimmed shrubs, and the flowering bushes.

As Nancy stopped the car at the front entrance, the door opened and Monsieur and Madame Bardot came out to greet them. At once the girls could see that Marie resembled her mother and Monique her father. The couple were most gracious in their welcome and led the visitors inside.

The furnishings were charming but not elaborate. They gave the chateau an atmosphere of warm hospitality, which was enhanced by vases of beautiful flowers.

The Bardots spoke perfect English, but upon learning that the girls could converse in French, Monsieur Bardot advised them to speak only in French during their visit. "I believe it will help you in your sleuthing," he added.

No further reference was made to the mystery at the moment, for suddenly excited barking came from the rear of the house. The next moment a miniature black poodle raced into the living room. She jumped up on the girls, wagging her tail briskly.

"Fifi! Get down!" Madame Bardot commanded.

"Oh, we don't mind," said Nancy. "She's very cute."

The girls took turns patting Fifi. When she finally became calm, Nancy said, "Monique told me that the dog sleeps in an antique kennel."

Madame Bardot smiled. "Actually, we should call it a bed, since we keep it in the house. Would you like to see it?"

She led the guests across the center hall into a combination library and game room. In one corner stood the most unusual dog bed the Americans had ever seen. The square frame, surrounding a blue satin cushion, was of gilded wood with an arched canopy of blue velvet. The headboard was covered in blue-and-white-striped satin.

"This was built in the early eighteenth century," Madame Bardot explained.

"How darling!" Bess commented. "Does Fifi really sleep in the bed? It looks so neat."

Monsieur Bardot laughed. "Every time Fifi comes into the house she is brushed off and her feet washed!" His eyes twinkled as if he were teasing his wife, who pursed her lips in pretended hurt.

The visitors' baggage was brought in, and the girls were shown to Marie's and Monique's bedrooms. They loved the wide canopied beds and dainty gold-and-white furniture. Bess and George said they would share the same room.

Conversation during luncheon was confined to Marie and Monique and their trip to the United States. Nancy told about the madrigal singing and how the people of River Heights loved it. The Bardots beamed with pride.

When the meal was over, their hostess arose. "Shall we go out to our patio?" she suggested.

The Bardots led the girls to the rear of the chateau and through a garden filled with roses, mignonettes, and summer lilies.

As soon as the group was seated in comfortable lawn chairs, Madame Bardot leaned forward. "Now please tell us, Nancy, have you had any success with my sister Josette's mystery?"

Nancy had decided it would be wise not to mention her father's case and had instructed Bess and George not to. She and the cousins described the various warnings received by Nancy, the helicopter incident, and the Aubert twins.

"I think," Nancy went on, "that Claude, the one in the United States, left the warnings at the request of his brother Louis."

"And," said Bess, "Louis calls himself Monsieur Neuf."

George put in, "We thought we had found the 99 steps but we were wrong."

"We may have a new clue to them," Nancy added. "Do you know of an orange garden in this area?"

After some thought, Monsieur Bardot replied, "At Versailles a double flight of steps leads down from a terrace to L'Orangerie, the orange orchard."

"You mean," Nancy said eagerly, "that there are 99 steps in them?"

The Frenchman smiled. "Actually there are 103 in each flight, but they are called the *Cent-Marches*."

"The hundred steps!" Nancy exclaimed.

"That's close enough to 99," George declared.

"It's worth investigating," Nancy agreed.

Her host suggested the girls drive to Versailles that very afternoon. "I'm sorry that my wife and I cannot accompany you, but we have an engagement."

Within an hour the trio set off. When they reached the palace of Versailles, Nancy parked the car and the girls walked up to the huge, sprawling edifice. They went to the beautiful gardens at the south side, exclaiming over the pool, palms, orange trees, and velvety grass.

Nancy spotted the imposing double staircase

leading down from a broad terrace of the palace. Excitedly the girls mounted the steps, counting them.

Presently Bess gasped and called out, "Look!" *On the 99th tread was a black chalk mark—M9!*

"M9—Monsieur Neuf!" George exclaimed. "Then what you overheard at Leblanc's last night, Nancy, was true! Louis Aubert must have come here. But when and why?"

"Maybe," Bess spoke up, "it has nothing to do with Louis Aubert after all."

Nancy shook her head in disagreement. "I believe Aubert chalked this M9 here as the spot where Monsieur Leblanc was to leave something —probably money. Let's do a little sightseeing in the palace and then come back in case Leblanc stops here on his way home."

The girls went down the steps again and walked to the main entrance. Inside, they stared in wonder at the grandeur of the palace. Walls, ceilings, and floors were ornate, but what amazed the girls most was the lavish decor of Louis XIV's bedroom.

"It's absolutely magnificent but it sure doesn't look like a man's room," George said.

"At least not a modern man." Nancy grinned. "Don't forget, back in the seventeenth and eighteenth centuries this was the way people in power liked to live, men as well as women."

When the girls came to the famous Hall of

Mirrors, a guide told them it was here that the peace treaty between the United States, England, and France on one side and Germany on the other had been signed after the First World War.

"They couldn't have picked a more beautiful spot," Bess murmured.

When the girls left the palace, Nancy glanced at her wrist watch. Very soon Monsieur Leblanc might be stopping at L'Orangerie. The three friends went back to the steps and waited. Minutes dragged by.

Finally George said, "I can't stand this inactivity another second. Nancy, I'm going to climb these steps again."

The next instant George was running up the flight of steps. When she reached the 99th, George stared in amazement, then turned around and called down to the others:

"The M9 mark is gone!"

The words were barely out of her mouth when she noticed a door in the palace being opened. No one came out, and she wondered if the girls were being spied upon.

"I must find out!" George said determinedly as she sped across the terrace.

Just as she reached the door a man's arm shot out. In his hand was a cane with a large curved handle. Suddenly the crook of the cane reached around George's neck and she was yanked inside the building!

CHAPTER XII

The Red King Warning

As the door of the palace closed, Bess shrieked and Nancy gasped. George was a prisoner! Whose? And why?

"M9 has kidnapped her!" cried Bess. "What'll we do?"

Nancy was already dashing up the steps. She crossed the terrace and tried the door. It was locked!

"Oh, I must get in!" Nancy thought desperately. She turned to Bess, who had followed her. "You stay here and watch. I'll run to the main entrance and see what I can find out."

She sped off and tried that door. It, too, was locked!

Desperate, Nancy banged on the door panels as hard as she could. In a few minutes a guard came out.

"The palace is closed for the day, mademoiselle," he said, annoyed.

"But listen!" Nancy pleaded. "A friend of mine was forced inside by somebody near the top of the L'Orangerie steps."

The guard looked at Nancy skeptically. She knew he was wondering if she had suddenly gone mad.

"This is serious," she said. "I'm not fooling. Please! My friend is in danger!"

Suddenly the guard seemed to sense that perhaps Nancy was telling the truth. He admitted her, and together the two raced up a staircase and to the door in question. No one was in sight.

The guard gave Nancy a look of disgust. "I do not like people who play jokes," he said brusquely. "Now you had better leave. And quickly!"

Nancy was at her wit's end. How could she convince this man? Then her eyes lighted on a pale-blue button from George's blouse. She picked it up from the floor.

"Here's proof," she said to the guard, and explained where the button had come from.

"Then where is she?" he asked, now worried himself.

"We'll have to find out," Nancy replied.

She led the way, practically running from room to room. There was no sign of either George or her abductor.

"Maybe the fellow sneaked down one of the stairways and went out," the guard suggested.

As the two stood debating where to search

next, they suddenly saw a man in uniform dash from one of the rooms and head for the main stairway.

The guard with Nancy muttered, "Very odd. I am supposed to be the only one left on duty."

Nancy cried out, "That man may be a fake! Come on!"

They dashed after the uniformed figure, but by the time they reached the top of the staircase he was out of sight. A door below slammed.

Out of breath, the guard said worriedly, "The fellow has probably escaped. I hope he did not steal anything."

Nancy had a different idea—that the fugitive had grabbed George with the crook end of the cane. "He must have left my friend behind. We'll have to keep searching!"

Nancy and the guard pressed on. Presently they reached Louis XIV's bedroom and stood still in amazement.

George Fayne lay on the ornate bed asleep!

At least Nancy hoped that George was *asleep.* Fearfully she went toward her friend. Just as she reached the bed, George opened her eyes. She looked around wildly, murmuring, "Where am I?"

"Oh, thank goodness you're all right!" Nancy cried out.

The guard's expression was one of utter disbelief. For a moment he could only stare at George as if she were an apparition.

"George, how do you feel?" Nancy asked solicitously.

"I—I guess I'm all right," George answered shakily. "When something hooked around my neck I blacked out." She started to sit up.

By now the guard was thoroughly alarmed. "No, no!" he insisted. "Do not move. I shall call a doctor. And I must also inform the police at once." He hurried off.

George protested, but Nancy agreed with the guard and insisted that George lie still. It seemed an endless time before the man returned with a physician and two police officers. After examining her, the doctor said that George was all right but should rest. Then he left.

Suddenly George burst out laughing. "This is so ridiculous! I can't believe it really happened!" Between gales of mirth, she said, "Imagine me sleeping in Louis XIV's bed!" Finally Nancy, the guard, and the policemen were also laughing.

George's eyes became so filled with tears of merriment that she had to wipe them away. As she pulled a handkerchief from the pocket of her blouse, a folded sheet of paper fluttered to the floor. Nancy picked it up and handed the paper back to George. When she opened it, a strange expression came over her face.

"What's the matter?" Nancy asked.

"Somebody put this note in my pocket! It's another warning!"

The two officers instantly became alert. "What do you mean?" one asked.

"First I'll read the note," she said. "Then my friend Nancy can tell you the rest." George read aloud the typed message:

" *'You girls mind your own business or*
grave consequences will come to you!
The Red King' "

"The Red King?" the second officer repeated. "*Mais*—but who is he—this Red King?"

"That's a new name to us," Nancy answered the question. "Other warning notes have been signed Monsieur Neuf and the Green Lion."

She explained sketchily about Mrs. Blair's mystery which had brought Nancy to France. The officers said that they had never heard any of the names.

"Earlier today we noticed that on the 99th step of the stairway from L'Orangerie someone put M9 in black chalk," Nancy went on, and told the whole story of what had happened.

The officers and guard were impressed. All said that these pretty American girl detectives were brave indeed to undertake such risks.

Nancy inquired, "You are sure that none of you knows a man named Louis Aubert?"

The three shook their heads. One of the policemen asked, "Does he live around here?"

Nancy said she did not know his address. "We saw him in Paris twice—once he was dressed as an Arab. I suspect he's involved in this mystery, and that he's the man in a guard's uniform we saw running away from here a while ago."

"We will make an investigation," the officers assured the girls. One of them reached for the note. "And examine this for fingerprints. You will come to headquarters if necessary?"

Nancy smiled. "Of course." She told where they were staying.

"Très bien. Very good!"

George insisted that she felt much better. "Let's get back to Bess. She's probably frantic."

The two girls hurried to rejoin their friend. Bess was relieved and delighted to see her cousin safe, but horrified to hear what had happened.

When the girls reached home, the Bardots were very much worried by the girls' adventure. "It is quite evident this Monsieur Neuf knows you three are on his trail. He is getting desperate," said Monsieur Bardot. "From now on you girls must take every precaution." They promised they would.

That night after dinner Nancy asked the Bardots where Josette Blair had lived as a child.

"Only a few miles from here," Madame Bardot replied. "Would you like to see the place? I'll take you there tomorrow morning after church."

"Oh, wonderful!" Nancy exclaimed.

The journey took them through rolling, verdant country. There was acre upon acre of green pasture and farmland filled with a profusion of growing vegetables and flowers in bloom. It was late morning when they reached another attractive, old-time chateau surrounded by gardens.

In the front a man and a woman were busy snipping off full-grown roses. Madame Bardot turned into the drive and asked the couple if they were the present owners.

The woman replied pleasantly, "Yes, our name is Dupont. May we help you?"

The visitors alighted. After making introductions, Nancy explained that Mrs. Blair, a very good friend of hers, had lived there as a little girl. At mention of the strange dream, the Duponts were greatly interested.

"Ah, *oui*," said Madame Dupont. "I do recall that Mrs. Blair lived here when she was little, but we cannot explain the dream."

Nancy asked, "By any chance do you know her governess, who was Mademoiselle Manon?"

"We do not exactly know her," Monsieur Dupont answered, "but a woman did stop here about five years ago. She told us she had once lived here as governess to a little girl but had lost track of her."

"This is very exciting!" Bess spoke up. "Can you tell us where Mademoiselle Manon lives? Mrs. Blair would like to know."

"I'm sorry, but we cannot help you," said Madame Dupont. "At the time of her call she wanted to get in touch with Mrs. Blair but had no idea where she was. We could tell her only that Mrs. Blair had gone to the United States."

Nancy wondered if the couple could give any kind of clue leading to Mademoiselle Manon's present address.

"Did she happen to mention where she was going?" Nancy inquired. "Or where she might have come from?"

"No," Monsieur Dupont replied. "But she did say she had married. Her name is Mrs. Louis Aubert."

CHAPTER XIII

Schoolmaster Suspect

WHILE Nancy and the other girls were mulling over the startling bit of information about the governess, the Duponts' maid came from the house.

"*Pardon,* madame. I could not help but overhear your conversation about a man named Aubert," she said. "Perhaps I can be of some help to the young ladies."

Everyone looked eagerly at her, and Mrs. Dupont said, "Yes, Estelle?"

The maid, who was a little older than the girls, turned to Nancy. "I come from Orléans. I went to school there two years ago, and one of my masters was Monsieur Louis Aubert."

This statement excited Nancy still more. Was she on the verge of a really big discovery?

"Tell me about the man. Was he in his fifties?" she asked.

"Yes." Estelle described her schoolmaster in

detail. He certainly could be the Louis Aubert for whom Nancy was looking!

"Can you give me his address?" she asked the maid.

"I am afraid not, except I am sure his home is in Orléans."

"Did you ever meet his wife?" Nancy inquired.

Estelle shook her head. "I do not even know her name."

Nancy thanked the girl, saying, "What you've told us might be of great help." She also expressed her appreciation to the Duponts, who said they were very happy to have met the Americans and wished them luck in their search.

During the drive home, the entire conversation revolved about Louis Aubert. Bess remarked, "Do you suppose he's leading a double life—one as a respectable schoolteacher, and the other as a crook?"

"It certainly looks that way," George said.

Nancy suggested, "How about going to Orléans and checking?"

Everyone thought this a good idea. After an early breakfast the next morning the three girls set off, prepared to stay overnight if necessary.

Madame Bardot kissed them good-by, saying, "If your sleuthing in Orléans should take much time and you girls plan to stay, please phone me."

"I certainly will," said Nancy, "and let you know how we're getting along."

A short time later the girls' conversation turned to the city of Orléans and its place in history.

"From the time I was a child," said Bess, "Joan of Arc, the Maid of Orléans, was one of my favorite heroines."

George added, "The idea of a girl soldier appeals to me. What terrific courage she had! That much of her story I do remember well."

Nancy smiled. "I wish we had Joan on this trip with us. She was a pretty good detective, too."

"Imagine a young peasant girl saving her country!" Bess remarked.

"Yes," said Nancy. "Joan was only seventeen when she requested a horse, armor, and an escort of men from a French commander to help fight the English invaders."

"I'll bet he laughed at her," George remarked.

"He did at first," Nancy continued, "but finally consented. Joan also wanted to help put Charles VII, the Dauphin, on the throne at Reims, which was held by the English. Charles was a weak man and had little money."

"And still he wanted to be crowned king?" George asked.

"Yes. He didn't want the English to take over France," Nancy went on. "When Joan arrived at

Charles' castle and offered to help, the Dauphin decided to test the peasant girl's ability."

"How did he do that?" George interrupted.

"By slipping in among his courtiers and asking one of the nobles to sit on the throne. But he couldn't fool her—she showed up the hoax at once."

Nancy smiled, brushing a strand of hair from her forehead. "Joan glanced at the man on the throne, then walked directly to Charles and curtsied. Everyone was amazed, since she had never seen the Dauphin in person."

Bess put in excitedly, "Yes, and Joan claimed she had seen a vision of the Dauphin. That's how she knew him."

George wrinkled her brow. "Joan finally did succeed in getting the king to Reims, didn't she?"

"Oh, yes," said Nancy. "Charles gave her a sword and banner and troops. In 1429 she rode into Orléans and freed the city from the English. Then the king was crowned."

"Unfortunately," Bess added, "she was captured a short time later and burned at the stake for heresy!"

"And you know," Nancy concluded, "twenty-four years after Joan's death at Rouen she was declared innocent. Now she's a saint!"

The girls became silent, thinking about the brave peasant girl and viewing the lovely countryside of the Loire valley. The soil was rich and the air sweet with mingled scents of fruit and flowers.

Later, as Nancy pulled into the city of Orléans, Bess requested that they go directly to the famous old square called La Place Ville Martroi, where a statue of Jeanne d'Arc on horseback graced the center. Nancy parked on a side street, and the girls went to gaze at the figure in armor high on a large pedestal.

At that moment the girls heard music. "That's a marching tune," said George. "Wonder what's up."

A crowd had begun to gather in the square. Speaking in French, Nancy asked the man standing beside her the reason for the music. He said a small parade was on its way. Soon the square was filled with onlookers.

Again Nancy spoke to the man. "*Pardon,* monsieur, but do you happen to know a schoolmaster in town named Louis Aubert? I should like to find him."

He nodded. "*Mais oui,* Monsieur Aubert is the bandleader in the parade."

Nancy and her friends could have jumped in excitement. In a few moments the schoolmaster suspect would appear!

As the music came closer, the girls strained their eyes to see the beginning of the parade. Suddenly a small boy standing near Nancy found he was too short to see the parade. He jumped over the flowers and onto a section of bench that surrounded the base of St. Joan's statue. Like a monkey he clambered up the pedestal.

"Oh, that's dangerous!" Bess cried out. "He'll fall!"

The boy was just pulling himself to the top of the pedestal when Nancy saw one of his hands slip. Instantly she jumped onto the bench. "Hold on!" she called to the boy.

The lad clawed wildly at the pedestal, but lost his grip. With a cry he dropped into Nancy's outstretched arms. The shock knocked the two into the flower bed. Neither was hurt.

"Merci, mademoiselle," the boy murmured, as they got to their feet.

By this time the crowd had begun to cheer. Nancy was embarrassed, particularly when the boy's mother rushed up and threw her arms around Nancy. In voluble French she expressed her thanks over and over again.

Nancy smiled, freed herself gently, and made her way back to Bess and George.

"Great rescue, Nancy," said George. "But in all the excitement we missed seeing the beginning of the parade. The band has gone down another street."

Dismayed, Nancy's instinct was to run after the band and try to spot the leader. But that was impossible. Several policemen had appeared and re-

The shock knocked them into the flower bed

fused to let the bystanders move about until the entire parade had passed.

"It's a shame!" George declared. "Maybe we can catch up with Louis Aubert somewhere else."

Nancy sighed. "I hope so."

The man to whom Nancy had talked earlier turned to her and said, *"Pardon,* mademoiselle, I see you have missed your friend. Would it help for you to speak to Madame Aubert?"

"Oh, yes!" Nancy replied.

"She is standing in that doorway across the square."

Nancy caught a glimpse of the woman as the marchers went by. But by the time the square was clear and the girls could cross, Madame Aubert had vanished.

"We've had so many disappointments today," Bess said wistfully, "something good is bound to happen soon."

Nancy urged that they try to catch up with the band. The trio ran after the parade, but by the time they reached the line of marchers, the band was breaking up. Nancy asked one of the drummers where she could find Monsieur Aubert.

"He has left, mademoiselle," was the answer.

"Can you tell me where he lives?"

The man readily gave the Auberts' address, but he added, "I know they will not be home until this evening, if you wish to see them."

Nancy thanked him, then turned to Bess and George. "Would you like to stay here overnight?"

"Oh, yes!" Bess's eyes danced. "Orléans is such an intriguing place. Let's have a long lunch hour, then do some more sightseeing."

"The place I'd like to see next," said Nancy, "is La Cathedral St. Croix, where there's another wonderful statue of Jeanne d'Arc. Shall we go there after lunch?"

The others agreed, and the three girls walked to a delightful little restaurant, where they ate a fish stew called *macelote*. It was served with a frothy white butter sauce to which had been added a dash of vinegar and shallots. For dessert they had plum tarts, which, on the menu, were listed as *tartes aux prunes*.

The stout friendly owner came to chat with the visitors. "Today people do not eat much," he said. "Banquets in medieval times—ah, they were different. Once at the country wedding of a nobleman near here this is what was served." He pointed to a list on the back of the menu.

9 *oxen*	120 *other fowl*	
8 *sheep*	80 *geese*	
18 *calves*	60 *partridges*	
80 *suckling pigs*	70 *woodcock*	
100 *kids*	200 *other game*	
150 *capons*	3000 *eggs*	
200 *chickens*		

"Wow!" George exclaimed. Even food-loving Bess said the idea made her feel squeamish.

The restaurant owner was called away, and the girls left a few minutes later. They went back to the square to visit the cathedral. Though not considered so grand as Notre Dame, it was a beautiful edifice with spires and domes. What interested the girls most about it was the statue they had come to see.

The sculptor had pictured Joan of Arc more as a saint than soldier. She was not wearing a suit of armor as usual, but was dressed in a long simple white robe. Her hair was short—cut in a bob— and in her clasped hands was her sword.

"Isn't the expression on Jeanne's face marvelous?" Bess said.

Nancy nodded. "Serene and spiritual. The sculptor certainly caught the spirit of her life."

As the girls finished speaking, a voice behind them said, "*Bonjour,* Nancy. I thought I might find you here."

Nancy turned. "Henri!" she exclaimed. "*Bonjour!* Where did you come from?"

Henri Durant, grinning broadly, greeted Bess and George warmly. He said, "I phoned the Bardots and they said you three were coming here. I offered to do an errand in Orléans for my dad," the French boy added, "so he lent me his car. Nancy, I hope you and your friends aren't too busy to take a ride with me."

Bess and George graciously declined, but urged Nancy to go ahead.

"Are you sure you wouldn't like to come along?" she asked. The cousins said No, they would go at once to the hotel where they had decided to stay. Nancy handed her car keys to George and said she would meet them at the hotel later.

The group left the cathedral and Henri led Nancy to his car. "Have you found that Arab yet?" he asked. When she shook her head, Henri added, "I was in the post office here this morning and saw a man who looked like the one in the taxi."

"In disguise?" Nancy asked.

"No, in regular clothes. He was just leaving the stamp window."

"That's very interesting, Henri!" Nancy exclaimed, wondering if the man could be Louis Aubert, the schoolmaster. It certainly seemed plausible. "I'll find out tonight," she thought, then determined to enjoy the afternoon's outing.

Henri drove to an attractive area of the river and rented a canoe at Collet's boat dock. They paddled in and out of various small coves. Nancy was enchanted by the landscape, some pastoral, some wooded.

Her companion proved to be humorous and told of his life as a student at the famous Sorbonne in Paris. "Someday I hope to be a lawyer." He grinned. "Then I shall give you some mysteries to solve." Henri said Madame Tremaine had told him confidentially that Nancy was an amateur sleuth.

"I can't wait for your first assignment," she said, her eyes twinkling.

Time passed quickly and only the lowering sun reminded Nancy they should get back. As Henri pulled up to the dock, the owner said a telephone message had come for him. "You're Monsieur Henri Durant?" When the young man nodded, Collet told him he was to call his father the instant the couple landed. The man walked off.

Henri laughed. "My dad certainly guessed where I would be! Please wait here, Nancy. I will be right back."

Almost as soon as he had left, a rowboat slid out from under the dock and bumped the canoe. Startled, Nancy turned to look squarely into the face of a heavily bearded man. Instinct told her to flee and she started to scramble to the dock.

"Oh no you don't!" the man said gruffly. "You are trying to solve a dream. Well, I will give you something to dream about!"

Nancy started to scream, but the stranger reached up and covered her mouth with one hand. With the other he slapped her face so hard she fell, dazed, into the water!

CHAPTER XIV

Amazing Number 9

THE cold water shocked Nancy back to semi-consciousness, so she automatically held her breath while plunging below the surface. Rising again, she tried to swim but had no strength to do so.

"I—I must turn over and float," Nancy thought hazily, and barely managed to flip over. A drowsiness was coming over her. "I mustn't let myself go to sleep," she thought desperately.

By this time Henri was on his way back. Seeing Nancy floating motionless in the water, he sprinted to the end of the dock and made a long shallow dive toward her.

"Nancy!" he cried.

"I'm all—right. Just weak," she replied.

Henri cupped a hand under Nancy's chin and gently drew her to the shore. Here he put an arm under her shoulders and helped the wobbly-kneed girl to the boat owner's office. Monsieur Collet's eyes blinked unbelievingly, but he asked no questions. Instead, he poured a cup of strong coffee from a pot simmering on a gas plate.

Nancy drank the coffee and soon felt her strength returning. Finally, able to talk, she told her story. Monsieur Collet was shocked and called the police at once to report the bearded stranger.

Henri frowned. The incident, he told Nancy, seemed to tie in with his telephone message. His father had not called him. "Evidently this villain planned the whole thing to harm you, Nancy. I shouldn't have left you alone."

"Don't blame yourself," Nancy begged him. "And now, if you don't mind, I'd like to go to the hotel and get dried out. Henri, will you bring my handbag from the canoe—if it's still there."

Fortunately it was, and not long afterward Henri dropped the bedraggled girl at her hotel. "I will telephone you tomorrow to see how you are," he said.

"Thanks a million for everything," Nancy said, "and I'll let you know if I find that Arab!"

When she reached the girls' room, George and Bess began to tease her about Henri having dunked her in the river. But they soon sobered as Nancy unfolded her story.

"How terrible!" said Bess.

"It does seem," George remarked, "as if you

aren't safe anywhere, Nancy, and what did he mean about the dream?"

"I guess he found out somehow about Mrs. Blair's dream," Nancy replied. "Who can he be? Everything happened so fast I didn't notice anything but his whiskers."

"I'll bet they were false!" George declared.

Nancy's spirits revived after she showered and changed into fresh clothes. She insisted that they call on the Auberts directly after a light supper. The girls had a little trouble finding the couple's house, but at last they pulled up in front of a small bungalow. As they alighted, the trio wondered if they were finally to face their enemy Monsieur Louis Aubert!

Nancy's ring was answered by a man who was definitely not the suspect. She politely asked if he were Monsieur Aubert.

"*Oui,* mademoiselle. You wish to see me?"

"Yes, if you can spare the time. And I would also like to talk with your wife."

"Please come in. I will call her."

He led the girls from a hallway to a neat, simply furnished living room. Then he returned to the hall and went upstairs.

A few minutes later the girls heard descending footsteps of two people. They tensed. Were they going to meet Mrs. Blair's governess? Would she solve the mystery of the disturbing dream?

The schoolmaster and his wife entered the living room and he introduced her to the girls. Madame Aubert, slender and dark-eyed, wore a puzzled expression. "You wish to see me?"

"Yes," Nancy replied. "We were directed here by a former pupil of Monsieur Aubert's. Please forgive our unannounced call."

The woman smiled. "As a matter of fact I am flattered that you have come to see me. Usually our callers ask for my husband."

Nancy explained how the Duponts' maid had overheard the girls say they were looking for Monsieur and Madame Louis Aubert. "Estelle directed us here. Mrs. Aubert, by any chance, was your maiden name Manon?"

To the disappointment of Nancy and the cousins the woman shook her head. "No. May I inquire why you wish to know?"

Nancy explained about the Lucille Manon who had been Josette Blair's governess. "We are eager to find her so she can give us some information about Mrs. Blair's childhood."

The schoolmaster and his wife were sympathetic and promised if they came across any lead to the other Madame Aubert they would let Nancy know.

George spoke up. "Monsieur Aubert, did you ever happen to run across another man with your name?"

"Yes. I have never met him personally, but mail for him has come here by mistake."

Nancy at once recalled Henri's statement about the man at the post office. "You mean his mail came to your home?"

The teacher smiled. "I am well known at the post office. When any letters for Monsieur Louis Aubert arrive in Orléans without a street address, they are naturally delivered to me."

Nancy asked eagerly, "Was there a return address?"

Aubert shook his head. "No. That is why I opened the envelopes. Of course, when I found out they were not intended for me, I returned the letters to the post office."

"How were they signed?"

"There was no signature—just the initial C."

The girls exchanged glances. "C" might stand for Claude—Louis's brother!

Excitedly Nancy asked, "Could you tell me what the contents of some of the letters were?"

Aubert replied, "Ordinarily I would not remember, but these letters were unusual. They were written almost entirely in symbols and numbers. The number 9 was especially prominent."

The three visitors were elated. Surely they had stumbled upon a valuable clue!

Bess spoke up. "Have you received any of these letters recently, Monsieur Aubert?"

"No. None have come in the past two weeks."

During the conversation that followed, it developed that as a hobby the schoolmaster had studied a great deal about alchemy. At once Nancy told him that only recently she had learned a little on the subject and mentioned the Green Lion symbol in particular.

Her remark set Monsieur Aubert on a lengthy but very interesting discussion of the medieval science. He brought a portable blackboard from another room and with a piece of chalk drew a circle with a dot inside it.

"That was the symbol for the sun," he said.

Next, he drew a half moon on the left and on the right of the blackboard drew what he said was the alchemist's sign for it. The symbol looked like a quotation mark, only a little larger.

"In olden times alchemists and astrologers worked hand in hand. The positions of planets on certain days were very important. Metals and chemicals were named after heavenly bodies. For instance, mercury—which we use in the laboratory today—was named after the planet Mercury."

He sketched the symbol and Bess began to giggle. "That's a sassy-looking sign. It reminds me of a scarecrow with only a smashed-in hat on!"

Everyone laughed, then the teacher continued, "I translated one of Aubert's letters to mean, 'Turn all gold to silver quickly with mercury.' Very odd to correspond in this manner. The writer must also be interested in alchemy."

Nancy herself had exactly the same idea. Not

only was Monsieur Neuf the mysterious chemist, but his brother might be one also! But how did this connect either brother—or both of them—with Monsieur Leblanc's secret? Was the financier buying up the rights to some important formula concocted by the Aubert twins?

As Nancy was speculating on this, the schoolmaster took up his chalk again. "The story regarding numbers is really quite fascinating," he said. "Take the 9, which appears so frequently in that other Louis Aubert's letters. The number was considered a sign of immortality."

On the board he wrote $9 = 9$, and then the number 18. As if he were addressing students, the teacher went on, "The sum of digits in successive multiples of 9 are constant. For instance, if we take 18, which is twice 9, and add 1 plus 8, we get 9." He grinned. "Who can figure out the next multiple of 9?"

Jokingly George raised her hand. "I feel as though I were back in school," she said with a laugh. "The third multiple of 9 is 27. The 2 plus the 7 equals 9."

"*Trés bien,*" the schoolmaster said. "And, Mademoiselle Marvin, how about you answering next?"

"I never was very good at arithmetic," Bess admitted, giggling. "But I do remember that 4×9 is 36. Add the 3 and the 6 and you get 9!"

"Exactly," said Monsieur Aubert. "This is

true all the way to 90. After that, the sums become multiples of 9."

The girls were fascinated and would have loved to hear more, but Nancy said they had taken up enough of the Auberts' time.

"We've had a wonderful evening," she added, rising.

Twenty minutes later the girls were back in their hotel. While getting ready for bed, Bess remarked, "I still think Louis Aubert, alias Mr. Nine, has cast some kind of a spell over Monsieur Leblanc. All this alchemy business sounds like black magic."

George scoffed at the idea. "I think Monsieur Neuf is just a plain crook who's robbing Monsieur Leblanc unmercifully. All we have to do is prove it."

"A big order." Nancy knit her brow. "I feel what we must do now is find Lucille Manon Aubert. I have a hunch she is the key that will unlock at least one mystery."

The following morning the girls set out early for the Bardot chateau and two hours later pulled into the driveway. Madame Bardot herself opened the door. At once the girls detected a worried expression on her face and sensed that she had bad news for them.

"What is wrong, Madame Bardot?" Nancy asked quickly.

The Frenchwoman's voice quivered. "My darling poodle Fifi has disappeared!"

"Oh dear!" Bess exclaimed. "You mean she ran away?"

Madame Bardot shook her head. "Fifi was locked in our house and could not possibly have left it of her own accord. But somehow she has just vanished!"

CHAPTER XV

Missing Gold

"Poor Fifi!" cried Bess. "She must have been stolen!"

"But that seems impossible," said Madame Bardot. "Every window and door on the first floor was locked. If some thief did get in, he must have had a key. But where did he obtain it?"

"Do you mind if we make a thorough search of the house?" Nancy requested.

"Oh, please do. We must find Fifi!" Madame Bardot's eyes filled with tears.

The group divided up to hunt, but with no success. As time went on, Nancy became more and more convinced that some intruder had been able to enter the house. On a hunch that the dog might have been hidden, she began a systematic search of all closets but did not find Fifi. Finally the only place left was the attic tower of the house. There was a door at the foot of a stairway leading up to it. Nancy opened the door and ascended. At the top she looked about at the small square room lighted by a tiny window on each side.

"Oh!" she cried.

In the center of the floor on a faded rug lay Fifi!

Since the dog did not move at Nancy's approach, she was fearful the pet might not be alive. In a moment she realized Fifi was breathing, but unconscious. There was a strong medicinal smell about the animal, and she guessed the dog had been drugged to keep it from barking the alarm.

Nancy was angry. Who would do such a mean thing? But there was no time to think about this at the moment.

Taking the steps two at a time, Nancy hurried to the second floor and called out loudly, "Come quickly! I've found Fifi in the tower!"

Madame Bardot rushed from a bedroom. "Is she all right?" the woman asked worriedly.

"I think so," said Nancy, "but a veterinarian should see her as soon as possible. She's unconscious."

By this time Monsieur Bardot had appeared in the hallway. He offered to phone the doctor and the police while the others hurried to the attic. Bess and George were indignant also at the mistreatment of the poodle.

In a short while the veterinarian arrived. He

examined Fifi and declared that the intruder had injected a drug that produced sleep for a long time. "She will be all right, however," he assured Madame Bardot. "And I do not think she needs medication. Just let her sleep off the effects."

As the veterinarian was leaving, two police officers drove up. They talked briefly with the doctor, then began to quiz the Bardots.

"We have little to tell," Monsieur Bardot replied. "My wife and I heard no unusual noises last night." He introduced the American girls, singling out Nancy. "Mademoiselle Drew is here trying to solve a mystery. Perhaps she can be of some help to you."

Both policemen frowned, and Nancy felt sure that the suggestion was not a welcome one! Quickly she said to the officers, "I'm sure you won't miss any clues the intruder may have left. But if you don't mind, I'd like to do a little looking myself."

The policemen nodded stiffly, then said they wanted to see where the dog had been found. The Bardots led them to the tower.

After they had gone, George whispered, "Nancy, I dare you to solve the mystery before those policemen do! Bess and I will help you find some clues before they get back downstairs!"

Nancy grinned. "All right. Let's start!"

While the girls were searching the first floor,

Bess remarked, "Nancy, do you realize that several houses—or buildings—you've been in lately have been entered by an intruder?"

"That's right," said Nancy. "But in this case, I hardly think the person was out to find me or take anything valuable of mine."

"If he was," said George, "he certainly got fooled, because we were away and had our passports and money and jewelry with us!"

Nancy examined the outside kitchen door. It had a Yale lock, but when she tried the key, she discovered that it was hard to turn.

"This must be how the prowler got in," she concluded. "He tried various keys before he found the right one, and almost jammed the tumblers."

"He's just a common burglar then," George declared. "He probably stole things from the house."

By this time the police and the Bardots had reached the first floor.

George blurted out, "Nancy discovered how the intruder got in!" She explained about the lock, then added, "The intruder put Fifi to sleep so she wouldn't bark and awaken anyone. Then, to keep the Bardots from notifying the police right away if they found the dog unconscious, he carried her to the tower."

The two officers stared at the girls unbelievingly. Finally both grinned at Nancy and one said, "I must admit you do have a good detective instinct, Mademoiselle Drew, and your friend here too. Perhaps you three girls can give us some more help."

This time Bess spoke up. "Yes, we can. I believe Monsieur and Madame Bardot will probably find some things missing."

At once Monsieur Bardot went to the desk in his den. He yanked open the top drawer, then said, "Well, at least the burglar wasn't after money. The bills I had here in an envelope are intact."

Meanwhile, Madame Bardot had hurried upstairs to her room. In a moment the others heard her cry out, "They're gone!"

The policemen rushed up the stairway, followed by the girls and Monsieur Bardot. They crowded into the bedroom.

"All my gold jewelry!" Madame Bardot gasped. "Some of it was very old and valuable—family heirlooms!"

This second shock was too much for Madame Bardot. She dropped into an armchair and began to weep. Her husband went to comfort her.

"There, there, dear, do not let this upset you," he said. "Fifi is going to be all right, and you rarely wear the old jewelry, anyway."

His wife dried her eyes. By the time the police asked for a description of the missing pieces, she had regained her composure enough to give them a list.

Nancy asked if any other jewelry had been taken, and Madame Bardot shook her head. This set Nancy to thinking. The intruder must have been after gold only! She inquired if there was anything else in the house made of the precious metal.

"Some demitasse spoons in the buffet," Madame Bardot replied, "and a lovely collection of baby cups."

She rushed downstairs to the buffet and opened the top drawer. "The spoons are gone!" Pulling the drawer out farther, the Frenchwoman cried out, "The baby cups too—all of them! I had one that once belonged to a queen. It is priceless!"

The Bardots opened every drawer and closet in the house to examine the contents. Nothing else had been taken. The police made no comment, but took notes.

Nancy herself was wondering if the intruder had a mania for gold. Suddenly she thought of the Green Lion, and Monsieur Neuf—Louis Aubert!

"Is he the housebreaker?" she asked herself.

Nancy was tempted to tell the police her suspicions about the man but decided that without any evidence she had better not. Instead, Nancy decided to consult her father about her theory.

After the police had left, she put in a call to Mr. Drew and fortunately reached him at once. He listened closely to Nancy's account of her adventures and agreed with her that Louis Aubert was indeed a likely suspect for the chateau thefts. "He must have known Madame Bardot owned objects of pure gold. I hope they can be recovered," the lawyer said.

Nancy mentioned the strange letters which Monsieur Aubert the teacher had received in error. She asked her father if he thought the elusive Louis Aubert, assuming he was a chemist, wanted the gold to use in an experiment.

"Very probable," Mr. Drew answered.

Nancy's father said he had news of his own. He had learned that Monsieur Leblanc had recently purchased a lot of uncut diamonds. "The reason is not clear," Mr. Drew added. "It would not be feasible for him to have such a large quantity of stones cut for jewelry, and diamonds are certainly of no commercial value to him—they're not used in his factory work as sharp drilling tools."

Mr. Drew went on to say that Leblanc had served notice his factory was closing down in a month. "Of course his employees are in a dither."

"That's dreadful!" said Nancy. "Dad, what are you going to do?"

Mr. Drew sighed. "I don't seem to be making much headway, but I have invited Monsieur Leblanc to luncheon today. I hope to find out something without his becoming suspicious."

"Please let me know what happens," Nancy

requested, "and I'll keep you posted. I wish you luck, Dad. Good-by."

A short time later the Bardots and their guests sat down to luncheon. Suddenly Madame Bardot said, "In all the excitement I completely forgot! A letter came from Marie and Monique. They have some news of special interest to you, Nancy. Incidentally, everyone at your home is fine, and our daughters are having a wonderful time. I'll get the letter."

Madame Bardot arose and went to the living room. Presently she returned and handed the envelope to Nancy.

"Shall I read it aloud?" Nancy asked.

"Please do," Monsieur Bardot said.

The message for Nancy was near the end of the long letter. It said that the night police guard presently in charge of Claude Aubert understood French. The day before the sisters' letter was written he had heard the prisoner mumble in his sleep, "Hillside—woods—ruins—go Chamb—"

"Whatever does that mean?" George spoke up.

"It is only a guess on my part," said Monsieur Bardot, "but I think the "Chamb" could be Chambord. That is one of the loveliest chateaux in the Loire valley."

"I certainly will investigate," Nancy said eagerly. She recalled the reference in Mrs. Blair's diary to the haunted ruins of a Chateau Loire. Perhaps the girls would have a chance to go there, also. Nancy now asked if there were any special stairs at Chambord.

Monsieur Bardot smiled. "If you are asking me about 99 steps, I cannot tell you. There is a double spiral staircase which is architecturally famous, and for that type, unusually wide and ornate."

As soon as the meal was over, Nancy suggested she and the cousins visit Chambord. Bess and George were enthusiastic and eager to go. In case of an unexpected overnight stay, the three took along suitcases.

They climbed into the rented automobile and Nancy headed down the driveway. As she neared the street, Nancy noticed a car approaching and pressed the foot brake. To her dismay, it did not work. Her car moved on!

Quickly Nancy leaned over and pulled on the hand brake. This would not hold either! With a sinking heart she realized there was no way to stop her car. It rolled onto the road directly into the path of the oncoming vehicle!

CHAPTER XVI

Followed!

THE three girls sat petrified. There was nothing Nancy could do to avoid a collision. The other car was too close!

But with a loud screech of brakes its driver swerved sharply and managed to avoid a collision by barely an inch. Nancy's car coasted across the road and stopped against an embankment. The shaken girls murmured a prayer of thanksgiving.

The man at the wheel of the other vehicle had stopped and now backed up. "Are you *crazy?*" he yelled at Nancy, his face red with anger. Then he went into a tirade in such rapid French that the girls could catch only part of what he was saying. They understood enough to learn he had had a dreadful scare also. "I ought to have you arrested!" he shouted.

Nancy started to apologize but did not get a chance to finish. The irate driver put his car into gear and sped off down the road.

Nancy turned shakily to the cousins. "Do you realize how lucky we were?" she said.

"Sure do," George replied fervently. "What went wrong anyhow?"

Nancy told her that neither of the brakes would work. "I'd better move and not block the road." She steered slowly back into the driveway and stopped by rolling against the sloping edge.

The Bardots had seen the narrow escape from a window and now came rushing out. "Thank goodness you are all right!" cried Madame Bardot. "What happened?"

Nancy told them quickly and at once Monsieur Bardot said, "Did you have any trouble with the car this morning?"

"None at all. It worked wonderfully." She frowned. "I'm sure someone tampered with the brakes."

"But when?" Bess asked.

"Probably during our search in the house," Nancy replied. "I also think the person who did it was trying to keep me from investigating some ruin near Chambord, perhaps even the Chateau Loire."

"Whom do you suspect? Louis Aubert?" George put in.

"Yes," Nancy answered. "He probably came back here after the police left and eavesdropped on our conversation. When he heard what his brother had mumbled in his sleep and learned our plans, Louis decided he had better do something quick to stop us."

"He must be a good mechanic to know how to damage brakes," Bess commented.

Nancy reminded her that the man was supposed to be a scientist. If so, he probably had a technical knowledge of machinery. "A simple thing like letting air out of our car's tires wouldn't have delayed us long enough, so he chose something more important."

Monsieur Bardot hurried indoors to telephone a service station. He returned with disappointing news. "They can send a man to pick up the car, but they cannot have it ready until tomorrow. If they tell me there was sabotage, I will report it to the police."

Nancy smiled wanly. She did not say how bad she felt at having to give up the trip. Apparently the Bardots sensed this.

"You must take our automobile," their host offered.

"Oh, thanks, but I couldn't," Nancy said. "You might need it."

Madame Bardot smiled, saying they had many friends close by who would help them out in an emergency. "I think you girls are on the verge of making an important discovery," she added. "We want you to go to Chambord. Perhaps you will solve the mystery of my sister's strange dream."

Nancy finally agreed. The baggage was transferred to the Bardots' car, and once more the girls set off. Their recent harrowing experience was almost forgotten as the three gazed enchanted at the countryside on the way to Chateau Chambord. Due to a late spring, poppies still grew in profusion along the roadway and fields were dotted with marguerites and buttercups.

When they reached the town of Chambord, the girls soon realized why the main sightseeing attraction was the chateau. Nancy parked near it and the trio alighted, exclaiming in admiration and awe.

The castle-like building stood in the center of a park and was approached by a long walk. The main part of the building was three stories high and there were many towers. A pinnacle in the middle, shaped like a gigantic lantern, stood as high again as the chateau itself.

On either side of its main entrance, and at each corner of the vast front of the chateau, was a huge rounded tower that rose well above the roof.

"I can't wait to see the interior!" Bess exclaimed.

But at the entrance, a guard told them, "Sorry, mesdemoiselles. The last tour of the day is just ending."

Nancy glanced at her wrist watch. It was later than she had realized. Nevertheless, smiling beguilingly, she said, "Please, until the tour group gets back here, couldn't we look around just a little?"

The guard softened. "I cannot let you go by yourselves," he said, "but I will show you a few things."

He let them in, locked the door, and led them straight ahead. When the girls saw the double spiral staircase of stone they gasped in wonder. The guard said with pride that the design was a unique one.

"You have to see it to believe it," said Bess. "What period does it belong to?"

"The Renaissance. This staircase, and in fact the entire chateau, is one of the finest examples of Renaissance architecture. It was built by King Frances I. He was fond of hunting, and the woods here at that time were full of deer and wild boar. The monarch also loved art and brought it to a high degree of perfection in France."

The group climbed to the second floor and he showed them several rooms. The girls agreed with their guide—the decor, although ornate, was in excellent taste.

The man grinned. "You might be glad not to see everything here—this chateau has 440 rooms, 13 large staircases, and stall for 1200 horses."

Bess exclaimed, "Think of all the servants and gardeners and grooms King Frances I must have had to take care of his home!"

The guide laughed. "You are right, mademoiselle. But in those days, a king was a king, and he had to have an extensive retinue!"

Regretfully the girls followed him back to the first floor. At the entrance Nancy thanked the man for the "special" tour, then asked if there were any ruins on the property.

"No," he answered. "You can see this place is very well kept. There are, however, a couple of ruins in the town—and, of course, some are scattered around the countryside."

The girls decided to walk through the streets of Chambord. They had not gone far before Bess complained, "I have the strangest feeling we're being watched. It makes me nervous."

Nancy had paid little attention. She was too busy absorbing the atmosphere of the chateau town. But presently she became aware that two young boys had come from one of the houses across the street and seemed to be trailing the girls. Whispering to her friends, Nancy suddenly did an about-face. Bess and George did the same, and the three girls started in the opposite direction. The two boys stopped, and after a momentary conference, they also turned and once more kept pace with the girls.

"I'll bet they're purse snatchers," Bess said fearfully. "Hold on to your bags."

Nancy did so, but her mind was suddenly running in another direction. Hunting for the ruins

to which Claude Aubert had referred was like
looking for a needle in a haystack. The young
detective decided to concentrate first on learning
if there were a chemist in the neighborhood. If
so, he might be Louis Aubert!

Excusing herself, Nancy hurried into a phar-
macy. To her annoyance, the two boys followed
her inside! In a low voice she put her question
to a white-coated man who came forward.

But his answer could be heard by everyone in
the place. "I do not know any chemist who lives
around here. Why do you ask?"

Nancy thought quickly. She must think up an
excuse!

"I am interested in chemistry," she said. "And
I believe a brilliant chemist lives somewhere in
this vicinity."

Out of the corner of her eye, Nancy could per-
ceive that the two boys seemed to lose interest in
the conversation.

"I am sorry. I cannot help you," the druggist
said.

Nancy bought some hard candy, then left the
shop. When she reached the sidewalk, the boys
were standing halfway up the block, apparently
debating between themselves whether or not
to continue following the girls.

Apparently they decided not to and turned in
the opposite direction. For an instant Nancy was
tempted to ask them what they were trying to

find out. But she refrained. The boys might have been engaged as spies by some enemy of hers. "It would be better to leave well enough alone," she thought.

As the three walked back toward the main street, Nancy asked a passer-by if there were any interesting ruins outside town.

"*Oui*, mademoiselle," the friendly man replied. "Chateau Loire. I would advise you young ladies not to go there alone now. You had better take a strong male escort with you. The ruins are some distance from the road and the access is difficult. Besides, it is rumored that tramps are living among them."

Bess spoke up promptly. "Definitely we're not going there. Nancy, I can't let you take such awful chances. Your father would never forgive me and George."

The man to whom they were talking smiled. "Ah! *Oui!* A most sensible decision."

Nancy thanked him for the information and words of caution. She and her friends walked on to their car. Just as Nancy started the motor, a white sports sedan roared down the main street. The girls were close enough to catch a good glimpse of the driver.

"Monsieur Leblanc!" George cried out.

"It certainly is!" said Nancy, swinging the car into the road. "Let's follow him!"

CHAPTER XVII

Knight in Armor

In moments Nancy and the cousins were heading after Monsieur Leblanc. But he was driving at such terrific speed Nancy felt wary of trying to overtake him.

George did not seem worried. "Step on it!" she urged.

But Bess had other ideas. "If we have a blow-out, good-by to us," she warned.

Fortunately the road ahead was straight and Nancy thought she could keep the financier's white car in sight for a while. George remarked that Monsieur Leblanc might suspect he was being followed.

"Yes," said Nancy. "And if he does, he certainly won't go where he plans to unless it's on legitimate business."

The sports car sped on for several miles. Then, a short distance ahead, Nancy noticed a sharp curve. Monsieur Leblanc did not slacken speed and roared around it.

"I mustn't risk that," Nancy told herself, and slowed down enough to take the curve safely.

As they reached the far side of the turn, George said in dismay, "He's gone!"

"But where?" said George. "To meet Louis Aubert perhaps?"

Nancy stepped on the gas and drove for another few miles. Their quarry had vanished. "I guess it's no use," she remarked. "We've lost him!"

She concluded that Monsieur Leblanc must have left the main road not long after passing the curve. "Let's go back and watch for any side roads." She drove slowly and presently the girls spotted a narrow dirt lane through the woods. There were tire tracks on it.

"Better not go in there," Bess advised. "What would you do if you met somebody driving out?"

Nancy smiled grimly. "How right you are!"

She parked the car along the roadside, and the girls proceeded on foot down the rutted, stony path. The tire tracks went on and on.

Presently Bess complained that her feet were hurting. "This must be a lumberman's trail that nobody ever bothered to smooth out," she said. "Where do you suppose it leads?"

"I hope to a ruin," Nancy answered. "The one Claude Aubert talked about in his sleep. It could be the Chateau Loire."

A little farther on the girls stopped and stared. Before them was a tumbled-down mass of stone and mortar. It had evidently once been a small, handsome chateau. Little of the building was intact, but as Nancy and her friends approached, they saw one section which had not yet suffered the ravages of time and weather. The tire tracks ended abruptly, yet there was no car in sight.

"I guess Monsieur Leblanc didn't come here," Bess surmised. She looked around nervously, recalling the guard's mention of tramps.

Nancy did not reply. Her eyes were fixed ahead on a series of stone steps leading below ground level. She assumed they had once led to a cellar or perhaps even a dungeon!

"Let's do some counting," she urged, and took out her pocket-size flashlight. Bess and George followed her to the steps. Would there be 99?

Nancy descended, counting, with the cousins close behind. When they reached thirty-five, Nancy stopped with a gasp. About ten steps below, at the foot of the stairs, stood a knight in full medieval armor! He was brandishing a sword!

George exclaimed sharply and Bess cried out in fright. But Nancy boldly took another step down. As she did, the armored figure called in French in a high ghostly voice, "Halt! Or I will run you through!"

Bess turned and fled up the steps. Nancy and George stood their ground, waiting to see if the figure would come toward them. He did not, but again warned them not to advance. This time his voice seemed a bit unsteady.

At once Nancy became suspicious. To the surprise of the other girls, she spoke up calmly, "Come now, Sir Knight! Stop playing games!"

The figure dropped the arm which held the sword. He fidgeted first on one foot, then the other.

"Take off the helmet!" Nancy ordered, but her voice was kind.

The knight lifted the visor to reveal a boy of about twelve! Bess and George marveled at Nancy's intuition.

Smiling, Nancy asked the boy, "What is your name?"

"Pierre, mam'selle. I was only pretending. Do not punish me. I did not mean seriously to threaten you."

"We're not going to punish you," Nancy assured him. "Where in the world did you get that suit of armor?"

The boy said it belonged to his father, who let him play with it. "I knew about this old ruined chateau and I thought it would be fun to come here and make believe I was a real knight."

Bess, looking somewhat sheepish, came back down the steps. "You had me fooled, young man!"

Nancy added with a chuckle, "I guess you didn't expect visitors to see your performance."

*"Halt! Or I'll run you through!" the knight
cried out*

Pierre grinned and admitted he certainly had not. Now the girls asked him about the ruin and he told a little of its history. The place dated back to the fifteenth century and was not the Chateau Loire.

"Are there any other ruins near here?" Nancy queried.

The boy said there was one across the road, deep in the woods. "I guess it's Loire. But do not go there," he advised. "Funny things happen."

"Like what?" George questioned.

"Oh, explosions and smoke coming out of the ruin and sometimes you can hear singing."

"Singing?" Bess repeated.

Pierre nodded. "It is a lady's voice. Everybody believes she is a ghost."

"Who's everybody?" Nancy asked.

"Oh, people who wander around there to explore. Some of my friends and I have gone as close as we dare to the ruin, but something strange always happens. We have not been near it in a long while because our parents forbid it."

Nancy was intrigued by this latest information. She asked for directions to the mysterious ruin.

"You go about a mile up the road toward Chambord. If you look real hard, you will see a narrow lane which leads to the place."

"Thank you, Pierre. Have fun." Nancy winked at the boy. "Don't let Sir Lancelot come and overpower you in a duel!"

The girls left Pierre laughing, and set off once more in the car. Nancy drove slowly and finally they spotted the entrance to the lane, well camouflaged by low-hanging branches.

Nancy pulled over and parked. Then the searchers trudged through the woods. Again the way was rugged and bumpy. Projecting underbrush kept catching the girls' clothes.

"If Monsieur Leblanc came this way," said George, "he sure scratched up his car."

"I doubt that he stopped here," Nancy replied. "No tracks." Suddenly she asked, "What's the date?"

George told her it was the 17th. "Why?"

"I'll bet," replied Nancy, "that tomorrow will be an important day here. It will be the 18th. One plus 8 makes 9, the magic number!"

Bess's eyes opened wide with fear. "Please! Let's get out of here fast! We can come back tomorrow and bring the police."

But Nancy and George wanted to proceed. Nancy said, "We'll need proof, Bess, if we expect police help. We don't know yet that this is Monsieur Neuf's hideout. Are you willing to go?"

Bess gulped hard and nodded. The three girls walked on.

A few minutes later Nancy stopped short. "Listen!"

The cousins obeyed. Somewhere ahead a woman was singing softly! Nancy whispered,

"That's one of the madrigals Marie and Monique sang." An electrifying idea struck her. "Girls! The singer could be Lucille Manon Aubert, the governess we're trying to find! Her husband Louis might be here too!"

Excitedly Nancy started to run toward the singing sounds which seemed to be coming from the woods to her right. George and Bess hurriedly followed her.

"We're getting closer!" Nancy said, breathless with suspense.

CHAPTER XVIII

Dungeon Laboratory

THE singing ceased abruptly. Had the footsteps of Nancy and the cousins alerted the woman? A moment later the girls heard someone scrambling among the bushes ahead, but the underbrush was too dense for them to see anyone.

"Do you really think that was Lucille Aubert?" Bess whispered.

George answered, "If she had nothing to hide, why would she run away?"

"What puzzles me is," said Nancy, "if she is Mrs. Blair's former governess, how did she get mixed up with a crook like Louis Aubert?"

The words were hardly out of her mouth when George caught her friend's arm. "Look over there!"

Some distance ahead in a clearing on a hillside the girls glimpsed the corner of a tumble-down chateau. A woman had darted from the woods toward the ruin. She was a tall, slender, graying blonde of about fifty-five.

"Do you think that's the governess?" Bess asked.

"She's about the right age," Nancy replied. "Come on!"

The three girls dashed forward up the hill, but when they reached the ruined chateau, there was no sign of the woman. Was she concealed nearby or had she gone on through another part of the woods?

Suddenly Nancy said, "Perhaps we shouldn't have given ourselves away. The woman may have gone to warn somebody else that we're here. We'd better hide!"

"Oh yes, let's!" Bess begged. "I don't want to be caught off guard by that awful Louis Aubert."

The girls ducked behind a cluster of trees and waited for over ten minutes. There was not a sound except the chirping of birds. No one appeared. Finally Nancy said, "I guess it'll be all right to investigate now. Shall we see if we can track down a few ghosts?"

"I'm game," George answered, and Bess reluctantly agreed.

Nancy led the way in the direction the woman had taken. They did not see her, but Nancy was fascinated to discover a very steep flight of stone steps leading down into the basement of the chateau. Suddenly the girls became aware of a faint roaring sound coming from below.

Nancy was very excited. Intuition told her she had found the right 99 steps! "I must go down there!" she exclaimed.

George grabbed her friend's arm. "Not alone!" she said with determination.

Bess did not want to participate in the venture. "I think you're taking a terrible chance, Nancy. You know what you promised your father. And frankly I'm scared."

George snorted. "Oh, Bess, don't be such a spoilsport. This could be Nancy's big chance to crack the mystery."

"Tell you what, Bess," said Nancy. "We really should leave somebody on guard here at the top of the steps. Bess, suppose you stay. If anybody comes, give our secret bird whistle."

"All right, but don't go so far underground you can't hear me if I have to warn you."

Nancy descended the steps, counting as she went. George was at her heels. Farther down, the daylight grew dim. To the girls' amazement two lighted lanterns hung from the crumbling walls. Somebody *was* below!

When Nancy reached the bottom, she could hardly keep from shouting for joy! She had counted exactly 99 steps!

Ahead was a narrow corridor leading to a huge

old-fashioned wooden door. In the upper part was a small square opening containing parallel iron bars.

"This must have been a dungeon!" the young sleuth thought. Cautiously she and George peered through the barred opening. Nancy gasped. A medieval lab! Maybe it once had been an alchemist's prison!

The laboratory was fully equipped with an open furnace in which a fire roared, and there were numerous shelves of heavy glass beakers, pottery vessels, assay balances, crucibles, flasks, pestles, and mortars. At the rear were several long benches, one of which held bottles of assorted liquids.

What amazed the girls most, however, was a man in Arab garb standing sideways at one of the benches! Nancy and George glanced at each other. Was this Louis Aubert again in disguise? The light was too dim for them to be sure.

The girls watched the man intently. In his left hand he held a black chunk which the girls guessed might be charcoal. In his other hand he had a knife and was busy gouging a hole in the chunk.

Evidently deciding it was large enough, the Arab picked up a large nugget of gold from the bench and dropped it into the hole. Next, he opened a jar and with one forefinger took out gobs of a pasty black substance and filled the opening.

Immediately Nancy recalled the old alchemists' experiments with metals and wondered if the nugget were real gold. Watching closely, she detected a look of satisfaction on what little she could see of the man's face. Now he set the charcoal on the bench, walked to the rear end of the laboratory, and went out a door. Before it closed, Nancy and George caught a glimpse of a corridor beyond.

The girls were wondering what their next move should be, when they heard Bess give the secret birdcall. The sound came loud and clear and was instantly repeated. The double call meant:

Someone is coming. Hide!

"Hide where?" George asked in a whisper.

Without hesitation, Nancy opened the laboratory door and motioned George to follow her. She tiptoed across the room to several large bins holding logs and charcoal. The girls ducked behind them.

They heard footsteps descending the stairway and a moment later Monsieur Leblanc strode in! Immediately he reached up above the barred door and pulled on a cord which rang a little bell. Within seconds the Arab walked in through the rear entrance. He bowed and said in a deep voice:

"Monsieur, you are welcome, but are you not a day early? Tomorrow is the magic number day. But it is well that you came." Suddenly his manner changed. He added gruffly, "I cannot wait longer."

Monsieur Leblanc's face took on a frightened expression. "What do you mean?"

The robed chemist replied, "I have finished my last experiment! Now I can turn anything into gold!"

"Anything?" The financier grew pale.

"Yes. Surely you do not doubt my power. You have seen me change silver into gold before your very eyes."

Monsieur Leblanc stepped forward and grabbed the Arab's arm. "I beg you to wait before announcing your great discovery. I will be ruined. The gold standard of the world will tumble!"

"What does that matter?" the Arab's eyes glittered. "Gold! Gold! All is to be gold!" he cried out, rubbing his hands gleefully. "The Red King shall reign! And when everything is gold, the metal will no longer be rare and precious! The value of money will collapse." He laughed aloud.

Monsieur Leblanc seemed beside himself. "Give me a little time. I must sell everything and buy precious stones—they will never lose their intrinsic value."

The chemist walked up and down for several

moments. Then he turned and said, "Monsieur Leblanc, your faith in me will be profitable. Watch while I show you my latest experiment."

He picked up a bottle filled with silvery liquid which Nancy guessed was mercury. He poured a quantity into a large crucible.

"Now I will heat this," the Arab said, and walked over to the open furnace on which lay a grate. He set the crucible on it.

The chemist waited. When the liquid was the right temperature, he took the piece of charcoal from the bench and started it burning. Presently the man dropped the mass into the crucible.

Nancy and George never took their eyes from the experiment. Once George leaned too far out beyond the bin, and Nancy pulled her back.

Blue flame began to rise from the crucible. The Arab placed a pan on a bench near the furnace, then picked up the crucible with the tongs and dumped its contents into the container. The charcoal had disappeared, and out of the mercury rolled the lump of gold!

Monsieur Leblanc cried out, "Gold!"

George looked disgusted, and Nancy said to herself, "That faker! He has Monsieur Leblanc completely bamboozled. Why doesn't he see through the trick?"

Both girls had a strong desire to jump up and expose the whole procedure. But Nancy was afraid the swindler would break away from them, and decided that it would be better for the police to arrest him.

Monsieur Leblanc seemed to be in a daze, but presently he pulled a large roll of franc notes from his pocket and handed them to the Arab. "Take these, but I beg of you, do not make your announcement yet. I will come at this same time tomorrow with more money."

"I will give you twenty-four hours," the Arab said loftily. "This time the price of my silence will be five thousand dollars."

The demand did not seem to faze the financier. As a matter of fact, he looked relieved. He said good-by and left the same way he had come in. The Arab went out the rear door.

The two girls arose from their cramped position, hurried outside, and up the 99 steps. Bess was waiting anxiously at the top.

"We must run," Nancy exclaimed, "and notify my father immediately that Monsieur Leblanc is being swindled!"

CHAPTER XIX

Nancy's Strategy

It was bedtime when Nancy, Bess, and George burst in upon the Bardots. Twice en route Nancy had tried unsuccessfully to get her father on the telephone.

The couple could see from the girls' excited faces that something unusual had happened. Nancy quickly poured out the whole story, feeling that the time was past when she had to keep her father's case a secret.

Monsieur and Madame Bardot were shocked. "You think this Arab you saw in that laboratory is really Louis Aubert?" Madame Bardot asked.

Nancy nodded. "Something should be done as soon as possible. I don't want to call the police until I talk to my father and ask his advice."

She telephoned Mr. Drew, but found he was not in. The switchboard clerk at the hotel, however, did have a message for Nancy.

"Your father said to tell you if you should call that he tried to reach you at Monsieur Bardot's but received no answer. Mr. Drew is an overnight guest of Monsieur Leblanc."

"Thank you," said Nancy.

After she put down the receiver, the young sleuth sat staring into space. She was perplexed by this turn of events. Nancy had so hoped to alert her father that Monsieur Leblanc was being hoodwinked by an alchemist's trick! Had Mr. Drew also learned this? Or had he come upon another lead in the mystery of the frightened financier?

"I'd better try contacting Dad at once," she told herself.

She called Leblanc's number. A servant answered and said that both men had gone out and would not be back until very late.

"Will you please ask Mr. Drew to call his daughter at the Bardots' number," Nancy said.

"Yes, mademoiselle."

When Nancy reported this latest bit of news to her friends, the others looked puzzled. She herself was fearful that her father might be in danger —perhaps from attack by Louis Aubert! Resolutely she shook off her worry. Surely Carson Drew would not easily be caught off guard!

The three girls, after a late, light supper, tumbled wearily into bed. In the morning Mr. Drew telephoned Nancy. She thought that his voice did not have its usual cheerful ring to it.

"I'm leaving here at once," he told his daughter glumly. "I will come directly to see you."

A sudden idea flashed into Nancy's mind. "Why don't you bring Monsieur Leblanc along? I have some exciting things to tell you which I am sure will interest him too."

Nancy did not dare say any more for fear some servant might be an accomplice of Aubert's and be listening in on the conversation.

"I'll ask Leblanc. Hold the wire." The lawyer was gone for a minute, then returned to say that his host would be happy to see Nancy again. "He'll postpone going to his office until this afternoon."

When the two men arrived, Nancy greeted Monsieur Leblanc graciously. Then, excusing herself, she took her father aside. "Dad, tell me your story first."

The lawyer said he had tried diplomatically to impress Leblanc with rumors he had heard of the financier's transactions. "I told him that reports of his selling so many securities was having a bad effect on the market and that his employees were panicking at the prospect of his factory closing down."

Mr. Drew said Monsieur Leblanc had been polite and listened attentively, but had been totally uncommunicative.

"I can understand why!" Nancy then gave a

vivid account of the girls' experiences of the previous day.

When she finished, Mr. Drew said he could hardly believe what he had just heard. "This Arab alchemist must be captured and his racket exposed, of course. The question is what would be the best way to do it without tipping him off? I certainly don't want Monsieur Leblanc to be harmed."

Nancy suggested that they tell the financier the whole story from beginning to end. "Then I think he should keep his date with the Arab this afternoon and turn the money over to him as planned.

"In the meantime, Bess, George, you, and I could go with a couple of police officers and hide near the 99 steps. Then, at the proper moment, we can pounce on Louis Aubert, or whoever this faker is."

Mr. Drew smiled affectionately at his daughter and put an arm around her. "I like your idea very much, Nancy. I promised you a lovely gift from Paris. Now I think I ought to give you half my fee!"

Nancy's eyes twinkled. "Only half?" she teased.

She and Mr. Drew returned to the others and Nancy whispered to Madame Bardot, "Would it be possible for you to find errands for the servants outside the house so that nobody will overhear our plans?"

"Yes, indeed. I'll send them to town."

As soon as the servants had left, Mr. Drew said, "Monsieur Leblanc, my daughter has an amazing story to tell you. It vitally affects your financial holdings and perhaps even your life."

The man's eyebrows raised. "This sounds ominous. Miss Drew is such a charming young lady I cannot think of her as having anything so sinister to tell me."

Bess burst out, "Nancy's wonderful and she's one of the best detectives in the world!"

Monsieur Leblanc clapped a hand to his head. "A detective!" he exclaimed. "Do you mean to say you have discovered why I am selling my securities?"

Nancy smiled sympathetically. "I believe I have."

Then, as Monsieur Leblanc listened in amazement, she related the story of Claude and Louis Aubert. She told about the many ways they had tried to keep the Drews from helping Monsieur Leblanc, and finally how she and George had seen the financier come into the secret laboratory at the foot of the 99 steps.

"You saw me!" he cried out. "But where were you girls?"

When Nancy told him they had hidden behind the bins, he knew she was not inventing the story. Leblanc sat silent for fully a minute, his head buried in his hands.

Finally he spoke up. "To think I, of all persons, have been duped! Well, it is only fair I give you my story. In the first place, if this chemist is actually someone named Louis Aubert, I do not know it. To me, the man is Abdul Ramos. I never saw him in any other clothes than Arabian."

Monsieur Leblanc said that Abdul had come to his office one day a couple of months before and showed him several very fine letters from Frenchmen, as well as from Arabs, attesting to his marvelous experiments.

Nancy at once thought of Claude Aubert. He could very well have forged the letters!

The financier continued, "Abdul wanted financial backing for a great laboratory he planned to build. Because of the letters, and some experiments he later showed me, I was convinced he knew how to turn certain things into gold. Yesterday when I saw the solid gold emerge from the heated charcoal—" Monsieur Leblanc's voice trailed off and he shook his head gloomily. "How could I have been so foolish!"

After a pause the financier admitted what Nancy had already overheard—he had intended to sell all his holdings and put the money into precious stones. "Since gold is the standard for all currency in international trade, I really feared the economy of the world would be disastrously

harmed when Abdul's ability to transform sub-
stances into gold became known."

Mr. Drew remarked, "That explains the large
quantity of uncut diamonds you bought recently."

The Frenchman looked surprised but did not
comment.

Nancy spoke up. "Also, you figured that
diamonds would replace gold as the world
standard."

"Precisely. I realize now that my self-interest is
unforgivable. It was neither patriotic nor human-
itarian. Instead I've been unforgivably greedy.
Thank you for showing me up. This has been a
great lesson to me and I shall certainly make
amends for it."

George asked, "Monsieur Leblanc, what about
the number 9?"

He explained that Abdul Ramos knew a great
deal about astrology and the magic of numbers.
"He convinced me that on the 9th, 18th, and
27th days of each month new secrets were revealed
to him and he threatened to announce his discoveries to the world."

George next inquired if he had left money on
the 99th step at Versailles where M9 had been
chalked.

Monsieur Leblanc nodded. "I did not see Abdul
that day, but left the money there at exactly the
time he had told me—directly after lunch."

When Leblanc was told of George's experience, the Frenchman was shocked. "All I can say is I am very sorry. I was foolish to let that man control me and cause so much worry." He shook his head sadly.

Bess, too, had a question for him. "Is Abdul married?"

The financier shook his head. "I have never heard him speak about a wife."

Nancy had been mulling over Leblanc's remark that he had allowed himself to be controlled by Louis Aubert and would like to make amends. She described her plan for exposing the fake alchemist.

"I will be glad to cooperate in any way," said the Frenchman, and Mr. Drew nodded approval. Soon afterward, Monsieur Leblanc left for his office.

Late that day three cars converged on the chateau ruin in the woods near Chambord. One vehicle carried Mr. Drew and the three girls, another two police officers, Beaumont and Careau. In the third was Monsieur Leblanc. The first two cars were well concealed among the trees and the passengers proceeded cautiously on foot through the woods.

At the small clearing near the ruin, they paused until they were certain no one was around. Then they darted to the 99 steps. Again the lanterns were lighted. The group tiptoed down.

Nancy peered through the barred opening of the door. Everything inside the laboratory looked the same as the day before, even to the glowing fire in the open furnace. The grating lay over it and she wondered if Abdul planned to show Leblanc another experiment.

Softly Nancy opened the door and one by one the watchers went inside and hid themselves behind the bins. Ten minutes went by, then Monsieur Leblanc strode in. He tinkled the bell and in a few seconds the Arab came through the rear door.

"Ah, I see you are on time, monsieur," he said smugly, with a little bow.

The financier reached into a pocket and brought out a roll of bills. He did not hand them over at once, however, saying, "Do you agree to a waiting period in return for this?"

"Have I not always kept my word?" Abdul said haughtily.

Leblanc laid the bills on a bench and immediately the Arab snatched up the money and tucked it into a pocket.

"How much more time do you wish before I reveal my great work to the world?" he asked.

"At least a week," Monsieur Leblanc replied. "I have several big transactions I must complete first."

"A week?" Abdul repeated, and began to walk around the room.

Presently he paused at the door which led to the 99 steps. The hidden group could see him reach toward it and heard something click. Nancy wondered if he had used a secret latch to lock the door and why. Were they all in danger?

Suddenly apprehensive, she watched the Arab intently as he returned to the furnace. He gazed at the fire, then with a brisk movement picked up a small sack from a bench. He hastened to the rear door, opened it, and whirled about. His eyes held a menacing gleam.

"Leblanc," he cried out, "you have double-crossed me! I know you have spies hiding in this room because I followed you to the Bardots! But I shall not be caught. Everyone of you shall perish!"

Without warning, the Arab threw the sack onto the furnace grate, then backed out, slammed the door and bolted it from the other side!

CHAPTER XX

Surprising Confession

It took but the fraction of a second for Nancy and the others trapped in the laboratory to realize the danger they faced. The sack hurled onto the furnace might explode at any moment!

Instantly Officer Beaumont jumped from his hiding place and made a grab for the bag. Fortunately, it had not yet ignited. As a precaution, he dropped it into a pail of water which stood nearby.

By this time everyone else had jumped up. Nancy exclaimed, "We mustn't let that awful man Abdul get away!"

She started for the doorway through which the Arab had fled, but then remembered he had bolted it from the outside. Those in the room were prisoners!

Nancy collected her wits. First she thanked Beaumont for saving them all. He shrugged this off and said, "We will have to break down the door and go after that crazy fool!"

Suddenly Nancy stared across the room in horror. Monsieur Leblanc had collapsed and was lying on his back, apparently unable to get up. Bess had already noticed this and was searching in vain for fresh water to revive him. Frantically she dug into her dress pocket and pulled out a small vial of perfume. Bess held it under Leblanc's nostrils. He took a deep whiff and almost instantly sat up.

In the meantime, the two policemen and Mr. Drew were heaving their bodies against the rear door. There was a loud splintering sound and finally the door began to give way.

The second it crashed down, the officers scrambled out and dashed up the corridor. Nancy started to follow, but her father held her back. "Let those lawmen handle the job," he said. "Beaumont was right when he called the faker crazy. No telling what he'll do."

The young sleuth became agitated at the delay. But only ten minutes had elapsed when they heard footsteps and voices in the corridor. Everyone gazed out and in the dimly lighted area they could see the police officers returning.

With them were Louis Aubert and the grayish-blond woman!

"She was the one who was singing the madrigals!" Nancy exclaimed.

Those in the laboratory could hear the woman saying, "My husband is a great scientist! He could not do anything wrong!"

"We'll see about that," said Officer Beaumont. "Anybody who wears a disguise and cheats people out of money by pretending he can turn almost anything into gold has a lot to answer for!"

Carcau added, "To say nothing of threatening lives!" Madame Aubert said no more.

As the four entered the laboratory, Louis glared malevolently at Leblanc, Mr. Drew, and the girls. At first he would answer no questions, but when confronted with accusations from the financier, Nancy, Bess, and George, the would-be scientist broke down and admitted to engineering the holdup of Monsieur Leblanc as well as practically all of the other charges against him.

Bess, proud of Nancy's sleuthing, said, "He has confessed to just about everything you suspected him of—even the canoe incident and to hiring two boys to follow us and get information."

Nancy, too, was elated—not only at the capture, but also because her father's mystery had been solved. There were still a few questions in her mind which she now put to the prisoner.

"Your brother Claude forged the letters of recommendation which you showed to Monsieur Leblanc, didn't he?"

"Yes."

Aubert also revealed that it was Claude who

had written the letters about a helipad being built on the Drews' roof.

The young detective suggested that the various other happenings in River Heights had been Claude's work, while those in France were Louis's schemes.

"That's right. I suppose you'll get it out of me sooner or later how I knew about you Drews, so I might as well tell you. A servant at the Tremaines is a friend of mine. It was he who stole an invitation for me to the soirée. He used to eavesdrop on conversations and found out that Mr. Drew had been retained secretly to investigate why Leblanc was selling his holdings.

"I did not want my scheme ruined, so I sent Claude to the United States. With his ability to forge all kinds of documents it wasn't hard for him to enter your country under another name. Unfortunately your father had left. But he did learn that you were coming and he did his best to frighten you into staying home."

"You used lots of names besides Abdul," George said to him. "Monsieur Neuf, the Green Lion, the Red King."

Aubert admitted this, adding that Claude, too, had used Neuf and the "Lion" on the warnings to the Drews. The prisoner bragged, "I know a lot about astrology and the practices of ancient alchemists. That's what gave me the idea about the gold and using alchemists' symbols." The M9 chalk mark had been left by Aubert at L'Orangerie as the place for Leblanc to leave money, but he had rubbed it out upon spotting the girls there.

During the interrogation, his wife had been sitting on a bench, pale with shock. She kept daubing her eyes with a handkerchief and murmuring, "I knew nothing about this."

Nancy went over and sat down beside the distraught woman. The young sleuth had not forgotten she had a mystery of her own to solve!

In a kind voice Nancy asked, "Were you Mlle. Lucille Manon?"

"W-why, yes!"

"I'm a friend of Mrs. Josette Blair. You were her governess many years ago. She has a recurring dream that frightens her. We thought perhaps you could explain the meaning of it."

The woman looked puzzled. "I do not understand," she said. "I took care of Josette when she was only three years old."

"Her dream dates back to that time," Nancy explained, and told about the nightmare.

As Nancy finished speaking, the woman began to weep aloud. "Yes, yes, I can explain. In a way Louis was responsible for this. I suppose he has always mesmerized me—as he has Monsieur Leblanc. During the time I was taking care of Josette, he was a guest at a chateau where the little girl and I had been left for a short time while her parents were away."

"Louis and I fell in love, and as it was not considered proper for a guest and an employee to date, we had to meet secretly."

Madame Aubert went on to say that Louis had already come upon the ruin with the underground alchemist's laboratory.

"It became our meeting place. One day I had to bring Josette along. He did not want her to recognize him or to see the laboratory for fear she would tell others about it. Louis wanted to keep the place a secret until he was ready to reveal a great scientific fact to the world."

The ex-governess went on, "I thought up the idea of playing blindman's buff. I took Josette to the woods and then blindfolded her. After we had played the game a while, I led her here. When I told her she was going down steep steps, Josette became afraid. I said I would hold her hand and she should count. Of course she could not count very far, so I did the rest."

"And the total, of course, turned out to be 99," Nancy put in.

"That is right," Lucille Aubert answered. "Louis thinks the alchemist who built this place chose that number of steps because it's a multiple of 9, a magic number for alchemists. The chateau dates back to the fourteenth century."

The ex-governess continued, "After Louis and I had looked at his laboratory, we three went back up the steps. Josette was still blindfolded. Just as she reached the top, she lost her balance and started to fall. Louis caught her, but for a long time after that, poor little Josette used to cry out in her sleep."

"No wonder the 99 steps made such a deep impression on her," Bess remarked.

Madame Aubert hung her head. "Not long after the incident, Josette's mother discharged me. I guess she suspected I was responsible for scaring her daughter. A short time later Louis and I were married."

Her husband spoke up. "When I found out the Bardot sisters were going to the Drews' home, I eavesdropped at the Bardots a good deal. One day I heard Madame Bardot read a letter from Mrs. Blair about the dream and I decided to send the warning note to her. Claude carried on from there. My wife didn't know anything about it."

Nancy said she was sure that when Mrs. Blair heard the story, her nightmares would cease. Nancy expressed her sympathy to Madame Aubert for her present predicament.

At that moment Officer Beaumont walked over to them. "I'm sorry, madame," he said. "You must come with us for further questioning."

Tears rolling down her cheeks, the woman arose. But suddenly she turned and said to Nancy, "Remember me to Mrs. Blair and tell her I loved her dearly."

Nancy felt her own eyes becoming a little dewy. "I'll be happy to," she replied.

Louis Aubert was made to release the secret lock on the door leading to the 99 steps. Before mounting them, Nancy suddenly remembered one part of the mystery was still unsolved. She asked Beaumont, "Did you search the Arab costume?"

The officer admitted they had not. "Wait here!" he directed, then hurried back into the rear corridor. He returned holding the robe, turban, and false hair. Beaumont searched the various pockets the costume contained. As Nancy had suspected, Madame Bardot's missing gold pieces were hidden in several of them! After a search, the rest were found hidden about the laboratory.

Everyone looked at Nancy admiringly. The officers shook their heads and Beaumont commented, "Mademoiselle Drew, *vous êtes merveilleuse!*"

George grinned. "In other words, Nancy, you're the greatest!" Her words were to prove true again when Nancy met her next challenge in *The Clue in the Crossword Cipher*.

The Auberts were led away. Then Nancy beckoned the others to precede her from the laboratory. Smiling, they all exchanged knowing glances. The young sleuth wanted to be the one to close the door to the mystery of the 99 steps!